CASE WITH NO CONCLUSION

CASE WITH NO CONCLUSION

BY

LEO BRUCE

Academy
Chicago
Publishers

Published in 1984 by

Academy Chicago, Publishers
425 N. Michigan Avenue
Chicago, IL 60611

Printed and bound in the U.S.A.

Library of Congress Cataloging in Publication Data

Bruce, Leo, 1903–1980.
    Case with no conclusion.

    Reprint. Originally published: London: G. Bles, 1939.

    I. Title.
PR6005.R673C35   1984   823'.912   84-14556
ISBN 0-89733-117-6
ISBN 0-89733-118-4 (pbk.)

TO
BOB AND WINIFRED PARKER

Chapter I

I STARED gloomily at the piece of notepaper. Really there seemed no end to the ingenuous ambitions of my old friend Sergeant Beef. He had already hinted to me that he was thinking of retiring from his post as a country police sergeant, but I had never dreamed that the luck he had had in stumbling on the solutions to a couple of murder mysteries would lead him into anything of this sort. The notepaper was headed W. Beef, and underneath were these extraordinary words: "Investigations promptly executed. Estimates given. Secrecy, swiftness, security." On the right of the paper was a London address, and on the left a telephone number.

Poor old Beef! A picture of him in his blue uniform at once rose to my mind. His straggling ginger moustache which always looked as though it had been dipped all too recently in beer, his irregular teeth and his air of mild remonstrance, his slow movements and his stolid way of thinking, marked him at once as the type of policeman likely soon to be superannuated by a Force full of zestful public-school boys. That he should have kept his job at Braxham had surprised me, for his fondness for the local pubs was a byword. That he should have been the means of tracing two murderers was a miracle. That he should be able to earn a living as a private investigator was beyond all human credulity.

However, there it was, and his letter followed. Written across his inferior notepaper in his large sprawling handwriting I read that he would like me to call on him as soon as possible. Concerned for his wife, a plain and sensible woman whose only ambition had ever been a clean cottage, plentiful meals and a gossip with her friends and relations, I decided to call at the address given.

I arrived there one afternoon at about half-past two, those doldrums of the day when lunch is finished and half-digested and it is not time for the reanimating cup of tea. Mrs. Beef opened the door of one of those small, two-storied, black, brick-built houses that may still be found in unlikely back streets between Baker Street and Paddington. Children were playing down the road, and the little front doors and closely curtained windows marked this unmistakably as a street in which bus conductors, workmen, postmen, and perhaps shop-assistants, whose work was in the Edgware Road area, had been lucky to find a small house for themselves. It was the last place in the world to which anyone looking for a private detective would come, even in answer to an advertisement.

"Beef'll be round in a minute," said his wife. "They close at half-past two," she added significantly as she showed me into the small front room.

Here her own tastes were predominant—lace

curtains, Victorian furniture, heavily framed photographs, and Goss china.

"How is he getting on?" I asked.

"Oh, well," said Mrs. Beef, "it may give him something to do now he's retired. He's got a bit put by anyway, you know, and I don't see it does anyone any harm for him to call himself a private investigator. Though what he wants to get mixed up in murders for I don't know. I don't mind reading about them in the papers. But further than that I won't go."

"Has he had any cases yet?" I asked.

"Cases? No," said Mrs. Beef. "'Course he hasn't. But he's started spending money putting advertisements in papers and says something'll come along soon. I can't help thinking you're to blame, Mr. Townsend, writing up those other two affairs as you did into books. It's given him such an idea of himself. Though I told him you were laughing at him half the time."

"What we've got to remember," I said, smiling, "is that he did actually discover the murderer in each case."

"Oh, well. . ." said Mrs. Beef finally, "there you are. You never know. It's a funny business. . . ."

"Quite," I interrupted, before she should reflect that life was what you make it, or that you never could tell.

Just then the front door opened and in a moment Beef was with us. I had never seen him out of uniform before, for in the old days he had preferred his blue tunic which, he said, he was "used to, for playing darts." The sight of his bright blue serge suit and mauvish tie rather embarrassed me. He held out his big red hand.

"Glad to see you," he said without smiling; "there's several private things I want to talk about."

This last remark was evidently his delicate and tactful way of suggesting that Mrs. Beef should leave us, for she immediately walked out of the room.

"Beef," I began at once, "what on earth is the meaning of all this? Do you really suppose that you can make a private detective of yourself?"

"Make?" he said, "I'm a born detective. And you should know it if no one else doesn't. I remember that time when the milk was disappearing off the doorsteps soon after I'd started in the Force. The Superintendent said to me then that I was a regular sleuth. A regular sleuth, he said, and no mistake about it."

I sighed, for the old boy's vanity made him invulnerable to sarcasm or contradiction.

"But what about your cases?" I asked; "Mrs. Beef says that you've been spending money on advertisements and nothing's come to hand. How do you account for that?"

Beef sat down heavily in a plush armchair, pulled out his pipe and turned to me.

"That's just what I wanted to see you about," he said; "I don't mean to say nothing rude, but I can't help thinking that if anyone's to blame, it's you."

"Me?" I began indignantly, but he held up his hand.

"Yes," he said, "the way you wrote up those cases. It was almost as though you were trying to make a fool of me. I got the murderers, didn't I? What more do you want?"

"But, Beef," I said, "you know you were lucky..."

"There's no such thing as luck in this work," said Beef. "Didn't Stute say so himself when he came down from Scotland Yard? It's method, Mr. Townsend. My methods are simple, but they work. I don't believe in a lot of skylarking about with microscopes and using half the inventions of Scotland Yard to sort out a little bit of evidence what anyone could see through with half an eye in their head. And there it is. I've arrested these two, and all I got from you was remarks about my being a simple country policeman. Then the way you put my language into print won't do neither."

"But after all, Beef," I said, "I only reproduce your dialect as accurately as possible. You're not a true Cockney, and I went so far as to explain that you spoke as Cockneys spoke in the home counties."

"Dialect," said Beef disgustedly; "it's nothing short of personal the way you have it printed. You should read the newspaper critics. You saw what Mr. Milward Kennedy said. 'Tedious' he called it, the misspelling and that."

"If ever you have another case," I assured him, "and I have to report it, I promise you your language will go in with all its aspirates, and none misplaced."

"I'm not sure you're the one to report it," said Beef. "You don't seem to make much *of* my cases. Not what some of them do for their detectives. *Case Without a Corpse* never hardly got no notices at all in the newspapers. Not like Miss Christie, or Mr. Freeman Wills Croft. They do get taken notice of. All you got for me was a bit in the *Sunday Times*, and not a smell from the *Observer*. A couple of paragraphs in highbrow papers like the *Spectator* and *The Times*, and there you are."

"I don't know whether that's quite fair," I said. "What about Raymond Postgate in *Time and Tide*? He called me the 'thriller reviewer's comforter.'"

"Only because you try and sneer at the others as writes detective stories what sells hundreds of thousands more than whatever you will. Why can't you make me famous? Like Lord Simon Plimsoll and those. I'm just as sure to get the right man in the end, aren't I? See where it comes in when a real good case comes along what really might help me to build up a connection, I don't get it. 'Course I know the competition's there. There's hundreds of them after anything unusual. There was that nice little case the other day, for instance, that would just have suited me. Body found in a brewer's vat. And who got the job? Nigel Strangeways, of course, Nicholas Blake's detective. And what about that kidnapping business down at

Kensington? It would have been handy for me, but Anthony Gethryn was put on to that because he's got Mr. Philip Macdonald to write him up. Where were we, I'd like to know? Then again, what about Fashion in Shrouds? Lovely, that was. Murder in a fashionable dress-designer's in Mayfair. . . ."

"But, Beef, surely you're not going to suggest that you would have been the man to investigate that case? It needed delicacy, tact, *savoir faire*. It was obviously just right for Miss Margery Allingham's Albert Campion."

"But I shouldn't half have liked it," said Beef, "mannequins and that," and he gave me a gross wink. "I never have any fun. Doctor Gideon Fell got that interesting little business of the two corpses in a hotel, with John Dickson Carr to tell the story. Why, even my cousin does better than I do."

"Your cousin?" I asked.

"Oh, you didn't know there was another Sergeant Beef? Of course, he's only an assistant to John Meredith, but he gets some interesting cases too. And you know why? Because Francis Gérard writes them up, and not someone like you who's only thinking how he can make jokes at my expense. Yes, my cousin Matthew Beef was telling me the other day, 'William,' he said, 'what you want is a first-rate man to write your stories, like Mr. Gérard does ours. That Townsend's no good,' he said, 'he's trying to be clever half of the time.' You see what's being thought."

I coughed uncomfortably.

"No, it all comes down to the same thing: I'm wasting my time. I need someone who can show I've got brilliance, insight, intuition, psychology, and all those remarkable things the others are supposed to have—though they don't work out anything more difficult than I do. It's disheartening, that's what it is."

"I'm sorry, Sergeant," I said, because I couldn't really be angry at this absurd tirade. "If ever you should get another case we must see what we can do."

"Of course, I shall get another case," said Beef. "What do you think I've put advertisements in the papers and my name on that door? Don't you know what happens? A mysterious stranger comes up, hot and perspiring with anxiety, tells me his wife's disappeared, and Bob's your uncle. You ought to know."

"Well, let's hope it does happen," I returned.

"Though I don't know," added Beef, with heavy jocularity, "that I should be in a hurry to trace her. I should be more inclined to congratulate him, and leave it at that."

Chapter II

IT must have been a fortnight later when I received a 'phone call from the Sergeant saying that Mr. Peter Ferrers was due to come and see him at four o'clock that day.

"It's this Sydenham case," he added breathlessly; "his brother's charged with murder and he's come to me to clear him. What do you say to that?"

I said nothing very much, except to congratulate Beef on the opportunity, and to promise that I would join him in Lilac Crescent at three-thirty.

As I sat with him waiting I didn't much like the way that the case was already following the precedents. Here we were not five hundred yards from Baker Street expecting the inevitable ring. And when Mrs. Beef put her head in the door to say that our first customer was looking at the numbers outside, I felt no particular excitement.

"Customer," roared Beef, as his wife went out to the passage; "she ought to know better than that. Client's the word."

But the young man who was shown in would

have been the first to disclaim the pretentiousness of that title. He was perhaps twenty-eight years old, slim and fair, with an open intelligent face, and dressed inconspicuously. I was glad to see none of the inconsequential regalia that young men so often carry—badges in buttonholes, ties of some immensely significant design, shirts of some knowing colour, all implying that they belong to this school or that movement. Beef eyed him appraisingly, and his first words surprised me.

"I've met you before, sir," he said pleasantly.

"Really?" said the young man. "I don't remember it."

"Ah, but you will when I tell you," replied Beef, his face spreading into a good-natured smile. "Don't you remember that Darts Championship when you and another young fellow played me and George Watson in the semi-finals? I finished on a hundred and twenty-seven that night. Treble nineteen, double top, and double fifteen. Nice get-out, that was."

Mr. Peter Ferrers nodded amicably. "Oh yes," he said, "I do remember now."

"Still," said Beef, with an air of coming to business, "you didn't come here to talk about darts, did you? What can I do for you?"

"Briefly," said the young man, "you can save my brother from being hanged for the murder of Doctor Benson, which he certainly didn't commit."

"Ah," said Beef, pronouncing that non-committal

monosyllable as though he knew all, but would say nothing at this point.

"Perhaps you have read the case," went on young Ferrers. "The papers have already given it a title—the Sydenham Murder, it's called."

"I don't hardly think it's fair, the way they make stories out of real murders, do you, sir? It's poaching on the detective novelist's department, I think. Torso Mystery, Burning Car Case and that."

I was beginning to feel uncomfortable, and wondered what young Ferrers could think of Beef. However, the latter had pulled out the enormous notebook which had followed him from his police-force days, and prepared to take down the details.

"My brother lived in Sydenham," said young Ferrers, "in a house called the Cypresses; one of those big gloomy mansions built for rich Victorian city men. We were both brought up there. When my father died a couple of years ago my brother decided to stay on. I believe he had an offer for the site from a Building Society—I could never understand his not accepting it. For in spite of our associations with the place it was inconvenient, cold, and cheerless. However, he's a bit of a sentimentalist and wouldn't leave the home. On Thursday night, a fortnight ago today, he gave a small bachelor party to which he invited Doctor Benson, who had been our family doctor for years. He didn't actually bring us into the world, being a man of forty-five himself, but since he had set up his plate in Sydenham fifteen or twenty years ago he had attended my father and us. I should perhaps explain the relationship because I think it's an unusual one. I never very much cared for Benson, finding him intolerant, and of a brusque, almost brutal disposition. He had a small gymnasium at the back of his house, and I remember that when we were boys, he persuaded my father to send us round to spar with him, and I think he took pleasure in knocking us about. But he kept my father's confidence, and that, I suppose, accounts for my brother's keeping up the friendship."

"What about his wife?" broke in Beef suddenly and rather rudely. It was evident that he had read newspaper accounts of the case.

Young Ferrers looked up, and for the first time I noticed some emotion in his face, though I couldn't altogether define it.

"Mrs. Benson," he said slowly, "is a very handsome and a very charming woman. Benson married her five years ago, and it seems that the police pay great attention to the fact that my brother was supposed to have been his rival at the time. I should prefer to say no more about this. You can meet the lady yourself, and if she is prepared to answer questions, you can ask them."

There was a moment's silence, and then Peter Ferrers continued: "The other guests at dinner were Brian Wakefield, who is a friend and colleague of mine, and myself. I had been trying for some time to interest my brother in the paper I run, and had wanted him to meet Wakefield, who is my fellow-editor."

"What paper's that?" I asked.

"It's called the *Passing Moment*," said young Ferrers.

"Do you put bits about books in it?" asked Beef at once. "Because I don't remember reading nothing about either of my cases in a paper with that name to it."

"I'm afraid we're chiefly concerned with politics," said young Ferrers mildly.

"What kind of politics?"

"Oh, vaguely towards the Left," Peter Ferrers told him.

Beef nodded. "That means you're a bit on the Socialist side, then?" he said. "Well, I voted Labour myself last election. I mean, I wouldn't like to see nothing like what's going on in Russia in this country, but I couldn't stand one of these jumped-up dictators, holding his hand out as though he had something in it what he wanted to keep away from his nostrils."

And with that summary of his political views Beef seemed satisfied. I, on the other hand, examined young Ferrers with a new, and not altogether sympathetic, interest. I disapproved of his type, which, however idealistic, seemed to me to be a disturbing element. But I could see that Beef liked him.

"Perhaps," said Peter Ferrers calmly, "we had better return to the matter I came to discuss. We dined at eight, and at half-past nine I and Wake-field left. He lives in a little flat in Blackfriars—three rooms, which I told him might be offices, but which he has converted into quite pleasant living quarters, and claims that they are quiet at night and perfectly convenient. I then drove on to the big block of service flats near the Marble Arch, in which I live, reaching there, I suppose, at about half-past ten."

"Did anyone see you come in?" I asked.

"I said 'Good evening' to the porter," replied young Ferrers, "and asked him if anyone had called for me, as I was half expecting another friend to come round during the evening. He said that no one had been there, and I went to bed."

Already in my mind the beginnings of a possibility were forming.

"You won't mind if I ask you," I said, "whether there is a way out of your flat except by the front door? I'm visualizing the possibility of some accusation being made against you," I added pacifically.

Peter Ferrers seemed quite undisturbed. "There is a service lift at the back by which I sometimes come in and out, but it would not be possible to come in this way after eleven o'clock when the outer doors are locked. There is also a fire-escape, but it leads down into an open court out of which there is no exit without disturbing the people who live round it."

"When did you first hear of the murder?" I persisted.

"Duncan, the butler, rang me up at nine o'clock next morning, and I went straight down there. It appears that after I left two of the servants heard a violent quarrel between my brother Stewart and Doctor Benson."

I groaned. "There is always a violent quarrel," I said. "How can I expect to make a good story of Beef's cases, when they conform so closely to type?"

"I'm bound to admit," said Ferrers rather curtly, "that I'm less concerned wth your efforts at fiction than I am with the clearing of my brother's name."

"Quite right," approved Beef, "it's only natural. Go on, Mr. Ferrers."

"After a while my brother rang for Duncan, told him that he'd want nothing more, and that he would show Benson out himself. Duncan locked up everywhere, as was his habit, and went to bed. The other servants had already gone up. Nothing more was known until a housemaid came down in the morning and found the doctor's body in an armchair in the library where he and my brother had been sitting. He had been stabbed in the throat— apparently with a single blow which had opened the jugular vein. An ornamental dagger which my father had bought many years before in an antique shop, and which normally lay on the library table, had been used, and had been put back on the table beside the chair in which the corpse was. My brother's finger-prints were found on the dagger, and in the room itself only those left by the guests of the night before. My brother, of course, knew nothing about it. He had shown Doctor Benson out some time, he thought, between eleven and half-past, and had gone straight up to bed. He had heard nothing during the night, and was sleeping soundly when he was called the following morning. That is as much as we know for certain."

"The front door was locked when the servants came down in the morning, I take it?" asked Beef.

"Yes, as usual, by the Yale lock. It's not bolted, as my brother gives the servants all the freedom he can, and if the girls want to go to the cinema or a dance they come in that way."

"There was no sign of anyone having broken in anywhere?" asked Beef.

"None whatever."

"Who had latch-keys?"

"The butler, Wilson, the chauffeur-gardener, the cook, and the two girls."

"And you?" I asked.

Young Ferrers smiled. "No," he said, "I used to have one when I lived at home, but I haven't seen it for years. I've had no need for it lately anyway."

"Then it looks," said Beef, "as though either your brother isn't speaking the truth about showing Benson out, or someone that had a latch-key brought him in. Or else he had a latch-key himself."

"Yes, those are the three possibilities, I suppose," said Ferrers.

"Very funny. Very funny indeed," was Beef's solemn reflection. "I suppose the best thing we can do is to get down to this house and have a look round. What about going straight away?"

"Very well," said young Ferrers, rising with some relief.

"There's just one thing," said Beef, "which is important in any murder case, and I should say is more important in this one than usual. What time did the doctor say Benson was killed?"

"Well," said Ferrers, "he didn't give an exact time. He said that Benson must have died somewhere within an hour either side of midnight. That was as far as he could say."

Chapter III

Rain was falling gently, and it was already dusk when we climbed into Peter Ferrers's car. The shining grey pavements of Lilac Crescent were almost empty in the pause just before the stream of people began to flow from the offices around to the nearest Underground station, and the anonymous occupants of the street itself began to drop home in ones and twos. Ferrers pulled up the grey hood of the large, shabby touring car which he had left standing outside Beef's door, and started the engine.

Beef sat forward in his seat uneasily and watched the traffic.

"Lucky for you I'm not still in the Force," he said at last; "you don't let nothing past, do you? In the built-up area too."

Young Ferrers did not answer, but sat almost carelessly in the driving-seat with only one hand on the wheel. The car swung easily between trams and blocked traffic.

Soon the traffic thinned as we got away from the centre of the town and the car kept at an even steady speed. Beef was silent for a long time. Then suddenly he turned to Ferrers. "What did you say the name of this house was?" he asked.

"The Cypresses."

"Funny. I thought you said the cider presses. Just shows how the stomach interferes with the ear sometimes. That's psychology, isn't it?" he added, turning to me.

But Ferrers interrupted. We had just turned into a long, wide street lined on either side by a high wooden fence which the rain had made black and protective.

"This is the road," said young Ferrers; "the house is just up here on the left."

As the car slowed down I realized what had inspired the unattractive name of the place. Half a dozen tall trees stood inside the fence so that the house was not visible from the road. They were dark, unjoyous things, not at all like the green flames Van Gogh found them to be in his paintings. They hung like a gloomy backcloth, the light from the street lamps flattening them and the fence into one dark wall.

The front gate stood open and Ferrers drove straight in. The house that stood before us must have been built in the same period that Elizabeth Barrett Browning's father had designed and built that large half-Turkish palace in which he never lived. Large houses of this type always seemed to express something of their owner's revolt against the age he lived in, as though the only relief from the "big business" of the period was in the slight fantasy of its architecture.

Not that the Cypresses was at all fantastic. It stood cold and dark, respectably isolated in its own

ground, but the spread of its ground-plan was that
of a more pretentious age. Like Abraham, the Vic-
torians liked to feel that their seed would be as the
sand of the sea-shore—and they built their houses
accordingly.

In the light drizzling rain, and in the shadow of
the row of cypresses, the house had a complacent
look. Sodden ivy almost covered one side of it, climb-
ing half-way up the tower which stood guardedly at
one corner. The single lamp over the porch was too
feeble to keep the shrubs more than a few yards away
from the door, and they stood in a close, damp semicircle, well kept and trimmed, but aggressive in
their rootedness. A young elder grew close against the
wall, in a corner where the light could not reach it.

"Not much of a miner's dream of home," said
Beef, as we climbed out of the car and stood for a
moment on the sticky gravel of the drive. "Do you
mean to say your brother lived here because he
wanted to?" he added incredulously.

The elderly man who opened the door looked
surprised to see Peter Ferrers, but he said nothing
as we walked into the long tiled hall and he took our
coats. I had been prepared for almost any sort of
severity or extravagance in the interior of the house,
but the cold hall, with its dark blue-green tiles, was
a surprise. It was like a corridor in a municipal
council office, clean and almost disinfected. There
were no rugs on the floor and the walls were bare
and dull with their dim yellow distemper. A heavy
coat-rack was the only furniture—a lonely and

tortured tree, with its mahogany arms flat against the wall like slow dark rivers curving lazily in a level country. But Beef did not seem at all impressed.

"Well," he said briskly, "where did you find the body?"

Young Ferrers smiled faintly and led us across the hall. "This is the library," he said, "but I'm afraid you won't find much in here. The police have been over it pretty thoroughly."

"Ah," said Beef, "you never know. It's the little things what count." He paused, as though searching for the right phrase. "Now where was Doctor Benson sitting when they found his body?" he asked at last.

Young Ferrers pointed to an armchair. Across the leather of the back and down the inside of one arm there was a dark patch.

"Blood, I presume," said Beef. "Would you mind"—he turned to Peter Ferrers—"just sitting there for a moment—like you was the dead man? So's I can get a picture of the room?"

I knew what Beef was thinking. He wanted to reconstruct the crime in the well-known manner, and although I approved of the method for dramatic purposes I could not see what use it could be at the moment. He looked pensively at the seated Ferrers and fingered his moustache.

"Ah," he said at last. And he might have meant anything.

"The police took the dagger away," said Ferrers, as he rose self-consciously from the chair.

"Where was it found?" asked Beef.

"On the table, the maid said."

"Didn't you see it there, then?"

"No, the police had come by the time I got here and they'd taken it away for finger-prints. They said everything else was to be left exactly as it was."

"Who did see the dagger, then?"

"Well, there was the maid who found Benson, Wilson, the chauffeur-gardener, and Duncan."

"You know," said Beef, as he began to wander slowly around the room once more, "it's surprising the things what the police don't see when they look into a thing like this. To begin with, they don't just look around, they start straight away to look for something. So there's bound to be a little detail here or there they miss."

"*You* should know," I reminded him smartly.

He paused, as I said this, by the table on which had been found the dagger, and on which still stood two used glasses and a decanter. Beef picked up one of the glasses and sniffed loudly at the contents.

It was the sort of thing Beef would do, I thought. He was in the middle of investigating a stabbing case and he started off by smelling the inside of a whisky glass.

"What does it smell of?" I asked sarcastically.

"Whisky," said Beef promptly. "Good whisky too. Not that I hold with it much. All over and done with too quick for my liking. Still, everyone to his taste."

Ferrers, who had been smiling vaguely at Beef's "investigation" of the room, now interrrupted.

"I expect you'll want to interview the servants," he said.

"Oh, ah," said Beef, "I suppose I ought to. Would you mind sending them in? The girl who found the body would be the best one to start with."

As Ferrers left the room, Beef turned suddenly to me. "Here," he said sharply, "there's a bottle in my bag. Fill it up with the whisky from that decanter. Look sharp, before he comes back."

"But, Beef," I protested, "we can't steal his whisky. You can't walk into someone's house and just walk off with. . ."

"You do what I say," cut in Beef. "Never you mind what we can and what we can't do. I'll keep a look-out while you do it, and don't you say nothing to nobody about this—I'll tell you all about it when we get outside."

Reluctantly I did as Beef said, and began to empty some of the whisky into a bottle. When the decanter was about half empty I went to replace it on the table, but Beef saw me.

"All of it," he said; "don't leave a single drop there. And what's in the glasses too."

I had just time to put the bottle back in Beef's bag when there was a light tap on the door, and the girl came in.

"You wanted to see me?" she asked.

"Yes," said Ferrers, who had followed her into the room. "Sergeant Beef here wants to ask you a few questions about the murder."

The girl came across the room and stood facing

Beef. She seemed slightly nervous, and smoothed her dress continually as she waited for Beef to begin. Pretty rather than beautiful, she had small, almost perfect features, and fair wavy hair which was untortured by hot irons or electric currents. Probably she wore no hat out of doors, for there were strands of hair, bleached paler by the sun, which she had drawn back from her forehead into a wide, almost old-fashioned hair-clip.

Beef produced his enormous notebook and laid it on the desk in front of him.

"Do you remember what you did that night, the night Doctor Benson was murdered?" he asked.

The girl was picking nervously at her cuff with quick bird-like movements, and did not answer for a moment. "I went to bed early," she said at last; "it was quite soon afer Mr. Peter's car drove away—about a quarter to ten I should think it was."

"How did you know it was Mr. Peter's car?" asked Beef quickly.

The girl looked bewildered for a moment before she answered. "Well, of course," she said, "it might not have been, but it was the only car in the drive, so I thought it must be."

"Did you hear anything in the house during the night?" I asked her.

"No, I must have gone straight to sleep."

"And you didn't wake up until the morning?"

"Not till seven o'clock."

Beef scratched his head with his pencil as if he

were not sure what to ask next. "And then," he said weightily, "you found Doctor Benson."

The girl nodded. She seemed to have anticipated the next question, for her eyes widened slightly as she watched Beef licking his pencil to make a note. As I looked at her small pale face it seemed to me that though she was obviously thinking of the body of the dead doctor as she had found it that morning, she was, in reality, quite unaffected by the murder or the arrest of Stewart Ferrers. In an independent type this would have not been surprising, but she was so clearly the reverse of this. She was answering Beef's questions as she would tell anyone the time—a subject others might find interesting but which somehow left her completely untouched.

Beef finished his laborious note-taking and turned to her again. "Perhaps," he said, "you could tell us something about how he was lying and that. Tell us just what happened after you come down, and how you found the body in the chair."

The girl gave a quick glance at Peter Ferrers before she answered, and apparently reassured, she turned back to Beef.

"Well," she said, "I came down as usual about half-past seven to clean up before breakfast, and after I'd done the hall and dining-room I came in here. The armchair had its back to the door, and I thought to myself—there's that Doctor Benson slept here all night—I could see it was him because of the top of his head. It just showed over the back of the armchair, and I recognized the bald spot.

Well, then I didn't know what to do. I thought if I woke him up he might be cross with me, and then again if I didn't Mr. Stewart might not like the room being left. So I thought I'd better try and do the room without waking him up."

"Why were you frightened Doctor Benson might be cross?" I asked.

The girl looked quickly across at Ferrers again, and then said, "Because he always was cross, sir."

"He was always cross with you?"

"With all of us."

"Didn't you like Doctor Benson?" asked Beef.

"It wasn't exactly not liking him," answered the girl, "but he used to be rather short with us like. Anyway, we always kept out of his way if we could—all except Ed. . .all except Wilson, and he seemed to think he was all right."

"Ah," said Beef. "Go on, then. When did you see that he was dead?"

"I was trying to tidy the room without making a noise, and there were some books on the table. Just as I was going over to pick them up I saw the knife lying just beside them, all covered with blood. It gave me a bit of a turn, but I didn't think nothing serious had happened and I went round to pick it up. But before I touched it I saw the doctor and I must have made a bit of a noise, although I don't remember screaming, because the chauffeur was passing round the house just then and he heard me. So he came in, and when he saw the blood and that he took me outside."

Suddenly she turned to young Ferrers as if she could not really express herself to Beef clearly enough. "It was awful, Mr. Peter," she said, "what with the blood all over everything, and the way his head hung over on one side. There was a big hole in his neck and all his coat and the armchair was red. And there was a funny sort of smell in the room that made me want to be sick. At first I had thought it was just the windows being closed all night, but then when I knew what it was...a sort of warm salty smell."

Beef waited a moment before asking his next question, and then, as if gently leading her away from the memory of the body, he said, "How long have you worked for Mr. Ferrers?"

"Nearly a year."

"Do you like working for him?"

"We don't hardly ever see him," she said guardedly.

Beef nodded. "Now about this knife," he said. "You say it was lying on the table. What was there unusual about it that made you notice it?"

"Why, the blood," said the girl in surprise.

"What I mean is," persisted Beef, "that there wasn't anything unusual in it *being* on the table?"

"That's where it always was."

"What makes you so sure?"

"Well, for one thing," said the girl, "because Mr. Stewart was always playing with it. Always had it in his hand, he did. He'd call you up to tell you something what ought to have been done, and he'd sit there twiddling the knife till it fair gave you the creeps."

"She's quite right, Beef," broke in Peter; "the knife was always on the table. It was used for anything. We used to sharpen our pencils with it, and things like that. Father always used to say he'd have it blunted, but he never did."

Beef turned to the girl again. "Do you know," he asked, "when the knife was cleaned last?"

"Why, at eleven o'clock that morning, of course."

"Of course?"

"I always cleaned the knife every morning. All the metal-work had to be done regular. Mr. Stewart was very particular about it," answered the girl.

"This knife," he said slowly, "what did it look like?"

Peter Ferrers interrupted. "It was quite an ordinary sort of dagger," he said; "Father picked it up years ago at a little antique shop. The handle was rather well done, in ornamental silver. I should say the blade was about eight or nine inches long, and about an inch wide all the way down, ending in a sharp point. But I expect the police would show it to you if you're interested."

"That's all right," said Beef, "I was only wondering. Now,"—he turned again to the girl—"when you came out of the library, where was Wilson?"

The girl thought for a moment. "Well, first of all he came out with me," she said, "and then when he saw I was all right he called out for Duncan, and went back in."

"Did Duncan come straight away?"

"I passed him on the stairs as I went down to the kitchen."

"Now, there's just one more question I want to ask you," said Beef, leaning forward over the table. "Have you any idea what Mr. Stewart was doing all that day?"

"He went out soon after breakfast," said the girl, "and didn't come home again till about half-past six, when he went straight upstairs to change. After that he sat and waited for the gentlemen to come."

"In the library?"

"No, he sat in the drawing-room."

"So he never went into the library at all that day?"

"No, not after he had Wilson in there in the morning."

"All right," said Beef, "that's all." Then as the girl turned to go an idea seemed suddenly to strike him. "By the way," he said, "what's your name?"

"Rose," answered the girl, but gave no surname.

Then, as she turned to the door again, Beef leaned forward and quickly picked a cushion off the settee.

"Here," he said, "what's this?"

On the side of the cushion were two long parallel lines of dark red; obviously blood.

"I don't know," said Rose, "I hadn't noticed it before."

I took the cushion from Beef and examined it. It was evident that a knife had been wiped on it.

Chapter IV

DON'T you think," said Peter Ferrers, "that the butler would be the person whose information would be most likely to help you?"

"I don't know," said Beef slowly; "I never much cared for butlers. I've noticed there's nearly always one of them around when a murder's been committed, though. Well, I suppose we'd better have him in."

I was disappointed in Duncan. I had hoped for something new in butlers. A one-eyed butler, or a little loud-voiced butler, would have been a change, but Duncan was painfully in the tradition. By conforming to type, I felt resentfully, he would make my task of narrating the case as something pithy and original, far more difficult. True he had some odd habits with his artificial teeth, but these could scarcely be considered startling enough to provide the "copy" I required. He clicked them and made them jump in his mouth, then, apparently with his tongue, dislodged the plate, so that two teeth jumped out on you as you watched, then disappeared again like small white rabbits down a burrow. But his tall, grotesquely thin figure and cadaverous yellow face, his long bony fingers and narrow bald head reminded me all too plainly of Suspect Number Three in a dozen films and stories.

"Duncan," said Peter Ferrers in a gentle and kindly voice, "these two gentlemen are making an independent investigation of the case in the hope of proving that Mr. Stewart is innocent. I want you to tell them all you can."

Duncan seemed startled. Indeed, his thin eyebrows were lifted as though he were permanently surprised, forever expecting a shock.

"Certainly, Mr. Peter. Whatever little I know," he said.

"Did you serve the dinner?" asked Beef, breaking in on this with characteristic clumsiness.

"Yes, sir."

"How was their appetites?"

"About as usual, sir. Mr. Stewart never ate a great deal, but Doctor Benson was hearty at the table."

"And what was they talking about over dinner?"

"Politics, most of the time. Mr. Wakefield did most of the talking."

"Any arguments?"

"Discussion, sir, I should call it. Mr. Stewart was never much in agreement with Mr. Wakefield's ideas, which were apt to veer towards the Socialistic a little."

"You mean he was a Red?"

"I have no means of knowing his opinions exactly, sir, but Mr. Stewart found them too progressive for his liking."

"I see. How long have you been with the family, Duncan?"

"I was engaged by the late Mr. Ferrers soon after he was married."

"So you've known Mr. Stewart Ferrers and Mr. Peter Ferrers all their lives?"

"Pretty well, sir."

"Now," said Beef heavily, "I want you to forget for a minute that Mr. Peter's in the room, and tell me straight out, man to man, what you think of them."

"I couldn't possibly presume," began the butler, but Peter interrupted him:

"Go ahead, Duncan," he said shortly.

"Well, sir, they were both good sons and their father knew it. He thought the world of both of them, sir, and it upset everyone terribly when he died. Mr. Peter will remember how he stayed up with him to the last, and after the end too. The doctor was wonderfully attentive as well, sir."

"You're wandering from the point," said Beef; "I want to know about their characters."

"Mr. Stewart was the quieter, sir. He was a very temperate man, religious and that. I understand he's helped the church here a geat deal. Mr. Peter was a bit more lively, if you understand me."

"And Doctor Benson?" queried Beef.

Duncan's face clouded. "I have always understood he was a very clever doctor, sir. Old Mr. Ferrers had the greatest faith in him, and wouldn't have anybody else near him in his illness."

"Have you always worked in this house?"

"Yes, sir, it was when he bought this house that he engaged me."

"Had he any children, then?"

"Mr. Stewart was born then, sir. Mr. Peter—ahem—arrived a year later."

"Are you married, Duncan?"

I thought I detected a smile on Peter Ferrers's face.

"Yes, sir. I've been married five years."

"Late in life," commented Beef, "to tie yourself up like that. Does she live anywhere round?"

"Oh yes, sir. She's the cook. We met in this house."

I was beginning to feel impatient at these probings of Beef's, for really the matrimonial affairs of Duncan, and the past history of the Ferrers family, could scarcely be thought to bear on the matter of Dr. Benson's murder. But you have to be patient with Beef.

"To come back to this binge," said Beef.

"Binge?" queried Duncan, more startled than ever. His teeth jumped out and in again, and he leaned forward slightly.

"Well, dinner-party, then." Beef's manner had taken on a sort of swagger, as though it had pleased him to find at least one witness who was nervous even of him. And it seemed quite certain that Duncan really was nervous. "What time did they start?"

"They sat down to dinner at eight o'clock as usual. Mr. Stewart was very strict in the matter of times, sir. Just as his father had been."

"And finished?"

"They went through to the library for coffee, I should say, at about twenty-past nine, sir. I took them the coffee and brandy in there."

"Do you remember what they were talking about in the library?" asked Beef.

Duncan paused, glanced at Peter, and shifted his teeth. "Yes," he said quietly.

"Well, come on, what was it?" roared Beef.

Peter seemed to nod permission, and Duncan proceeded. "Well, it was about this periodical of Mr. Peter's and Mr. Wakefield's. I have heard it discussed before, sir. It seemed that Mr. Wakefield wanted Mr. Stewart to give it financial support."

Peter Ferrers broke in. "Yes, that's quite right, Sergeant," he said. "Wakefield and I are not rich men, and the *Passing Moment* is in pretty low water. We had been trying for some time to persuade my brother to subsidize it."

"Any luck?" asked Beef.

"He means," I interrupted hastily, "were you successful?"

Peter was quite good-humoured as he said, "I'm afraid not."

"So that's what you heard?" Beef asked Duncan.

"Yes, sir. Mr. Stewart was very definite. Not in any circumstances, he said."

"That's all?"

"That was the gist of it. There was nothing else of any importance I could gather."

"And then you went back to the kitchen?"

"Yes, sir."

"Who was there?"

"My wife and the two girls. My wife wanted to know if the dinner had been satisfactory, and when I told her that Mr. Stewart had complained about the savoury again she was very put out." Duncan shook his head, and his pale face seemed stretched by an expression of concern.

"What's she do when she's upset, then?" asked Beef, a grin beginning to show on his face.

Duncan remained dignified. "On this occasion she marched straight off to bed," he said.

"Leaving you and the two girls?"

"Yes, sir. But not for long. They was doing the crossword puzzle in the evening paper and Freda kept yawning, though I've told her before it's not manners. At about a quarter-past nine Freda went up; that wasn't long before Mr. Peter and Mr. Wakefield started off."

"You saw them go?" asked Beef.

"Oh yes. I went up and got their coats and hats."

"Did they seem all right?"

"Er—how do you mean, sir?"

"Sober, and that," said Beef.

Peter was again smiling when Duncan said, "Most certainly, sir. I've never seen any member of this family anything else."

"Good-humoured?"

"So far as I could gather, sir. They said good night to me."

"And you saw them drive away?"

"Yes, sir. I watched the car disappear down the

drive. When I got back to the kitchen, Rose was just going up to bed."

I was watching Duncan closely, and was not surprised to see that on the tight and parchment skin of his forehead a few drops of perspiration showed.

"And then?" said Beef relentlessly.

"Then, a little later, Mr. Stewart rang. I went up to the library and found him alone with Doctor Benson. He said I was to bring the whisky and soda, and needn't wait any longer. That's about all I know, sir."

"Half a minute, half a minute," said Beef, "we're just coming to the interesting part." He leaned forward and said in a slow, emphatic voice, "What was they talking about when you took the whisky in?"

Duncan seemed almost to tremble. "I explained that once to the police, sir," he said.

"Never mind about the police," said Beef; "you tell me. What was they talking about?"

"Well, as I crossed the hall, sir, I heard their voices raised. It seemed they were quarrelling."

"If you heard their voices raised," said Beef, "you must have heard what they said."

"Well, I did hear Doctor Benson say something which I didn't understand."

"What was it?"

"He said, 'It's in my surgery now.' "

"What else did you hear?"

"Nothing very clear, sir. But I gathered that

Mrs. Benson came into it. I heard her name mentioned two or three times."

"And how did her name come into it?" asked Beef.

The butler looked confused. "Really, sir," he said, "I should hardly know that. I suppose it was on account of Mrs. Benson and Mr. Stewart." He looked apologetically at Peter Ferrers as he said this, and there was a sharp rattle of teeth as the bottom set gave an unusually large jump.

"And what about Mrs. Benson and Mr. Stewart?" asked Beef heartlessly, for I could see that Duncan was more than usually embarrassed by this question.

"Well, sir, there was a story going around about there being some sort of an affair between Mr. Stewart and Doctor Benson's wife. People have seen them together, out in the car, and so on."

"Oh, they have, have they?" said Beef. "What people are these? Have you seen them together, Duncan? Or did you get the story from someone else?"

Duncan hesitated for a moment before replying. "I can't remember, sir, exactly who told me," he said. "Everybody knows about it, of course. But if I remember correctly, it was Wilson who first told me about them going out in a car together."

"All right," said Beef, "we'll leave that for a bit. But there's something which is important. Mr. Ferrers says he showed the doctor out at a quarter-past eleven. Did you hear him go?"

"No, I was asleep by then."

"You went straight to bed after taking up the whisky and soda?"

"Yes, sir. That is, of course, after I'd locked up everywhere."

"What do you mean, 'locked up'? Bolted the doors and so on?"

"Yes, sir. Mr. Stewart was very careful to have all the downstairs windows fastened—they all had special catches on them that you couldn't slip open with a knife—and also all the doors had to be bolted. All except the front door, which had a Yale lock and was left in case any of the servants stayed out late at a dance or the pictures."

"You're sure everything was done properly that night?"

Duncan looked slightly hurt, and his eyes took on an almost angry expression as he answered, "Everything was in perfect order, sir."

"And you were in bed and asleep when Doctor Benson left?"

"I was asleep by a quarter-past eleven, sir."

"But surely you would have heard his car drive away?"

"Possibly, sir, but he wasn't driving his car. He came on foot."

Beef looked at him at though he were angry. "And that's all you heard or saw that night, is it?"

"Yes, that's all."

"When did you first know he'd been done in?"

"When Wilson, the chauffeur-gardener, shouted

out for me next morning. I hurried upstairs to tell him not to shout about the house like that."

"Did you see the girl Rose?" asked Beef.

"Yes. It was from her I could see there was something wrong. I met her on the stairs—white as death she was. When I got into the library, there was Wilson standing staring at Doctor Benson. 'He's been murdered,' he said."

"Had you seen Stewart Ferrers that morning?"

"Yes, sir, I took his tea in at eight o'clock as usual."

"He seemed all right?"

"Oh yes. He was asleep when I got into the room. He said good morning, and drank his tea as he did every day while I handed him his paper."

"And there's nothing you can tell us? Not about the past or anything?"

Duncan was already shaking his head before Beef had finished his question. "No, nothing at all," he said, and Peter signed for him to leave the room.

"He knows more than ever he'll come out with," was Beef's comment.

"What makes you think that?" asked Peter.

"Ah," said Beef.

Chapter V

"WELL," said Beef expansively, "I don't know what you gentlemen feel, but. . ."

I hurriedly interrupted, for I knew what proposal he was about to make. "You'd better interview the chauffeur-gardener," I said severely.

He gave me a vicious look. "All right, have him in," he sullenly conceded.

Wilson was in his chauffeur's uniform, and stepped into the room smartly. He was a good-looking fellow, tanned and well built. But his manner was a little too slick and ready for him to be, in my mind, completely trustworthy. He seemed quite at his ease and more than ready to answer any question that could be put to him, as though he were almost enjoying the situation.

"Sit down, Wilson," said Peter Ferrers. "You can smoke if you like," and he handed him a box of cigarettes.

Wilson thanked him, lit one, and blew two columns of smoke through his nose like a picture of a dragon in a child's book.

Beef gaped at this performance, then seemed to pull himself together for his cross-examination. "What did you think of this Doctor Benson?" he began unexpectedly.

"Well, I found him all right," said Wilson, "though he wasn't popular round here at all. Bit of a bully, I should say. But he never tried any of that stuff on me."

"Had you had any dealings with him, then?" asked Beef.

"Not what you could call dealings. I've driven his car round to the garage when he came to the house, and once or twice taken some plants up from the garden to his place."

"So you do the garden, do you?" Beef asked him. "I never cared for gardening," he continued to us all contemplatively; "thirsty work I call it."

"I like it all right, but Mr. Ferrers wasn't really interested. I didn't have enough time to keep the place as I wanted."

"You remember the day before the murder?" asked Beef, "and everything that happened on it?"

"Well, not everything, but I've got it fairly clear in my mind. I always come in at eight o'clock for breakfast, and it was then he sent for me and asked me if I could do with my evening out that day instead of the following Monday, as he wanted to go to the theatre on Monday evening."

"Anything unusual about that?" asked Beef.

"Unusual! I should say it was. It's the first time I'd ever heard him mention a theatre. I've often said I'd have liked a job with someone who got up to the West End a bit more. Other chauffeurs get a couple of hours in the evening to knock about where it's a bit livelier than down here, and I never have a look in."

"Oh," said Beef, "that's your type, is it? Want to go gallivanting round the West End every night?"

Wilson glanced at me, and returned, "No, not that exactly. But I want to see things, get somewhere. You feel, in a place like this, that you're buried alive, except on your day out. I don't want to be a private chauffeur all my life. I'd like to have a garage of my own."

"Well, you're not likely to get it by 'opping in and out of West End bars where they charge you ninepence for a bottle of pale ale. However, you was to go the theatre on the Monday. Go on."

"Mr. Ferrers just asked me if I minded changing my day out, and although I wasn't very pleased, I agreed."

"Why weren't you very pleased?" asked Beef sharply.

"Because on my day out I usually go to my sister's place, and I wasn't sure she'd be there if she wasn't expecting me till Monday."

Beef made some of his painfully slow notes, and then looked up to say, "Is that all he said to you?"

"No, he asked me some technical questions." Wilson's manner implied that this would be out of the scope of a mind as simple as Beef's.

"Technical questions, eh? What about?"

"About pre-selection gears."

"And what might those be?"

"They're a kind of gear change without a gear-lever. That's as simply as I can put it."

"Never mind about putting it simply," said Beef; "had his car got 'em?"

"No, his was an Austin."

"Whose had, then?" asked Beef.

Wilson smiled and drew slowly at his cigarette as though he knew that his reply would be impressive. "Doctor Benson's had," he said; "it's a Lanchester Ten."

Beef's pencil scratched again. "And that's all that Mr. Ferrers said to you?"

"Yes, that's all."

"Did you take your evening off?"

"I did."

"What time did you leave?"

"Oh, threeish," said Wilson.

Beef looked up and spoke irritably. I knew privately that the fact that the pubs had now been open for half an hour was telling on his patience. "If you mean three o'clock," he said with solemn dignity, "perhaps you'd be good enough to say so."

Wilson remained unruffled. "Well, about three o'clock," he said.

"How did you go? By bus, or what?"

"No, I went on my motor-bike."

"Oh, you've got a motor-bike, have you? Dangerous things. I always used to tell young Galsworthy, who was the best young policeman I ever

had under me, that sooner or later he'd break his
neck. Flying round the country like someone gone
mad. But these young fellows will never pay no
attention to caution. So you went on your motor-
bike. Where did you go?"

"To my sister's home in Edgware."

"What time did you get there?"

"I went straight there; I don't know what time it
was."

"Did you see your sister?"

"No, she and her husband were out: gone away
for the week-end."

"To a house-party, I suppose?" said Beef sarcastically.

"No, to Southend," said Wilson.

"So what did you do?"

"Had some tea with the landlady, and sat talking for a bit. She told me that if I wanted to stay the
night, as I usually did when I went over there, I
could do so."

"Why should you want to stay the night?"
snapped Beef suspiciously.

"It's a long way to Edgware," said Wilson, "and
the roads are clearer early mornings, I always
think. Besides, when I'm out, I never want to get
back to this place sooner than I can help."

"I see. No attractions here, then," leered Beef.

"What exactly do you mean?"

"Well—there's two young girls in the house, you
know."

Wilson made no reply, but lit another cigarette.

"Did you stay the night, then?" Beef queried.

"Yes."

"What did you do all the evening?"

"Went to the pictures."

"What, alone?"

"Yes. Why not?"

"Never thought of taking the landlady, I suppose?"

"What, her? No thanks, she's fifty."

Beef grew sarcastic again. "And ladies over twenty-five wouldn't be expected to enjoy the cinema, I suppose?" he said. "What film did you see?"

"*Little Miss Broadway*," replied Wilson, without any hesitation at all, "with Shirley Temple."

" 'Orrible," commented Beef, shaking his head. "What was the name of the cinema?"

"The Super-Titanic," said Wilson.

Beef bent over his notebook, and mumbled as he wrote, "Confirm film at cinema on date," then looked up again. "Did the landlady let you in?" he asked.

"No, she'd gone to bed."

"How did you get in, then?"

"By opening the door with a key," said Wilson with patient sarcasm.

"How did you get the key?"

"The landlady gave it to me."

"And when did you leave there?"

"About seven o'clock next morning."

"Did you see the landlady again?"

"No, she wasn't up. I left the key on the kitchen table."

Beef looked at the young man fixedly. "Have you any way of proving, then, that you did stay the night in Edgware?"

Still there was nothing startled in Wilson's manner. He thought for a minute, and then said, "No, I suppose I haven't. But I did stay there all the same."

Beef grunted. "Go on with when you got back to the house," he said.

"Wait a minute, there is a witness who'd prove it," suddenly remembered Wilson. " An old chap I met as I was coming in the drive. I was just turning in on the motor-bike when I saw him. He looked as though he might have been out all night, and he came trotting along with a walking-stick in his hand."

"From the house?" asked Beef attentively.

"Well, I don't know if he'd come from the house itself, but he was coming out of the drive."

"Had you ever seen him before?"

"No, I can't say I had. He was probably just a passing tramp."

"Would you know him again?"

"Yes, I think so."

"Is there anywhere he could have been in for a doss?" asked Beef.

"There's the summer-house; he might have been in there."

"All right. Carry on," said Beef.

"I was working in the garden before breakfast," continued Wilson, "when I heard Rose, the housemaid, give a sort of scream in the library."

"What do you mean, a sort of scream?" asked Beef.

"Well, half a scream if you like," said Wilson.

"So what did you do?"

"Hurried indoors and went through to the library. The girl had just found Benson murdered. She was pretty well knocked out, of course, and I took her out of the room and called out to Duncan, then went back. It was enough to upset any girl. There was a lot of blood; nasty sight altogether."

"How long was Duncan in coming?"

"Oh, a few minutes. I don't know exactly."

"And that's all you know?"

"That's all I know," said Wilson.

I felt I'd like to know a little more about this young man, and in spite of Beef's impatient snapping of his notebook and movements towards departure, I turned to him.

"What sort of education have you had?" I said to him.

"Pretty ordinary. I went to a Technical School."

"You don't seem upset by all this."

"Well, it's not exactly my affair, sir."

"Not that your employer has been charged with murder?"

"He was my employer. He didn't mean a great deal to me personally. In fact, I scarcely knew him."

"What does mean a great deal to you personally, if one may ask?"

"Getting on," said Wilson, without any hesitation. "Being someone, seeing something of life."

I thought how much I disliked the type, but left it at that. But Beef had remembered another point.

'Here," he said as the chauffeur stood up to go, "what was this story about Mr. Stewart and Mrs. Benson? What do you know about it?"

"Only what everybody else does, I suppose," answered Wilson.

"And what was that?"

"People have seen Mr. Stewart and Mrs. Benson out in the car together, or at a dance, or going to the theatre. Everybody knows about it."

"Where have you seen them together?" asked Beef.

"Well, I can't say that I have."

"Who told you about it, then?"

"I believe it was Duncan—couldn't say for sure, but I think it was him."

"Oh, it was, was it?" said Beef, but rather to show he had his own opinions on the matter than to ask another question.

Peter Ferrers, however, did not seem hurt by Wilson's carelessness. "All right, Wilson," he said, "you can go. I'm sure you'll tell us if anything useful occurs to you."

"Yes, sir," he said, and walked out as smartly as he had entered.

"What about the cook and the other housemaid?" I asked, but Beef had made up his mind.

"Not today," he said pointedly. "I've had enough for one day. They'll be expecting me back near my home. I'll be down again tomorrow, Mr. Ferrers, to carry the investigation a stage further."

It seemed to me that Peter Ferrers had more trust in Beef than I had. He was smiling as he said, "Do you feel that you're getting anywhere, Sergeant?"

"Oh, just inklings here and there," said Beef as he picked up his hat. "It'll all come out in time."

Chapter VI

N EXT morning I was dozing comfortably in bed thinking over the stray ends of evidence which we had accumulated on the day before. I had formulated no theory yet, and I did not think that Beef had. But I felt that the police must have some good reason, of which we knew nothing, for having arrested Stewart. If Stewart were not guilty, then it seemed to me already that there were a number of people on whom suspicion could fall. The four who had slept in the house beside Stewart, Duncan, the cook, and the two housemaids, must not be excluded, however unlikely they seemed. Wilson had no alibi after some time early on that evening, and he had a motor-bike on which it would have been possible for him to reach the house. Peter himself could have returned in his car. And what had the old tramp been doing whom Wilson had met coming out of the drive in the morning? I made a note in my mind to tell Beef to find out whether the police had discovered at what time precisely Benson had been murdered, and I wondered whether he was also following up the possibility of the tramp having something to do with it.

Just then the telephone bell rang, and I lifted the receiver to hear Beef's voice. "There's a development," he said.

At that time in the morning his pompously bookish phrases were rather irritating, and I asked him sharply what had happened.

"That old carcase as we were interviewing yesterday..."

"Do you mean the butler?" I asked.

"That's him," said Beef, "he's done himself in."

"What?" I sat up in bed.

"Yes," said Beef, too stolidly for my liking, "they found him this morning. Hanged himself in the scullery he had. They found him in his night-shirt."

"But why?" I asked.

"Well, he happened to be wearing it at the time, I suppose."

"I mean, why did he commit suicide?" I asked impatiently.

"That we hope to know in due course," said Beef. "What time will you be round here?"

"As soon as I'm dressed," I promised.

"Well, no need to hurry," said Beef, "I haven't shaved yet. The missus has gone out to get some kippers for breakfast. Peter Ferrers has only just rung up to tell me. It means the police will be down there this morning. I wonder what they'll think of me being on the case?"

"You seem to take this man's tragedy very calmly," I said.

"Well, *I* couldn't help it, could I? See you later."

And he put the receiver down.

I dressed quickly and scarcely stopped for breakfast, for however indifferent Beef might be, I began to see this case as genuinely unusual. But when I reached his house I was disappointed to hear from Mrs. Beef at the door that the Sergeant was still having his breakfast.

I found him at work on his kippers. Whatever clichés could be used for Beef, no one could say that he "toyed with his food." If he could have dissected motives and situations as thoroughly as he did those smoked fish, he would have been a great detective. In spite of my impatience, I was fascinated by the process, and sat watching until the third one was a bleached skeleton on his plate, and he had swallowed his last cup of tea.

"Ah," he said, filling his pipe, "there's nothing like a kipper."

"But, Beef," I began, "you can't hang about like this. That man's suicide may mean anything in the case."

"And it may mean nothing," said Beef. "We shall soon find out when we get there. Now come along. Have you brought your car?"

"Yes," I said.

"Then drive around to Suffolk Street, Strand."

"Suffolk Street, Strand?" I said, for quite apart from my rôle as the perpetually astonished observer, I was genuinely at a loss to know what he was up to this time.

"That's what I said," he returned as he climbed

into my Ford Eight. And rather than give him the satisfaction of seeing that I was mystified, I drove where he told me in silence.

When we stopped at the number he mentioned, I found he had brought me to the offices of the *Passing Moment*, the paper which belonged to Peter Ferrers and Wakefield.

Beef clumped into the outer office and asked the girl whether Brian Wakefield was in.

"What name?" she said.

"Beef," said the Sergeant, as though he was mildly astonished that she shouldn't already know.

"From Mr. Peter Ferrers," I added.

We were kept waiting some five minutes, and then shown into a room on the door of which were the words, *Editor, Private*, conspicuously painted.

Wakefield was sitting at a big desk facing us as we entered. He did not look up but showed us the top of a large head while his pen continued to move over the paper in front of him.

"Sit down," he murmured, still writing, and rather sheepishly we did so. Beef, however, soon became impatient and began a series of throat-clearings which would have been sufficient to disturb Wakefield had he been genuinely at work.

Suddenly he laid down his pen and looked up, and before either of us could even greet him, began to speak.

"You've come to hear what I know about the Ferrers business. If you will just sit perfectly quiet I'll tell you in as few moments as possible—no, don't interrupt. I have learned to make myself coherent, and I can give you the facts in a far more concise form that you could possibly extract them by questions."

He was standing up now, with his hands thrust deep in his trousers pockets. He must have stood six feet four or five, and his slight stoop and his very large head gave him an overshadowing aspect. His voice had the rich complacency which goes with culture in Oxford and good living in London. He wore a blue serge suit, and his black Eden hat hung behind him. I knew his type well. Intellectually talkative, self-confident, and rather useless. I had met men of his category patronizing the assistants of West End bookshops, contemptuously "putting at ease" visitors to Broadcasting House, leaning over bars in places which were, for some reason, called exclusive. His face was flattish, with cheeks which went straight up to his eyes so that there was no pocket under them, or lashes on the under-lids.

"First of all, about this family," he said, "though there's nothing very remarkable about the history. Peter and I were at school together, and I've been in and out of that mausoleum of a house since I was twelve. The mother was a nice, ordinary little woman, and the father a pleasant old sentimentalist. I've never liked Stewart, and should think he probably did the murder."

The last sentence was spoken casually, as though Wakefield wished to imply that it didn't seem a very important matter to him who had committed the murder, or how many murders had been committed, and that we were a couple of mildly contemptible fools to bother about the thing at all. Beef, however, tried to interrupt at this point.

Wakefield raised his hand. "I don't say he did," he went on, "because I always find evidence, and that sort of thing, rather boring. But he was perfectly capable of doing it if he felt it incumbent upon him. He was one of those people who've never really established their relationship with the world. He lived on an island of little ideas. A dangerous man in a sense. He was desperately fond of money, though, and worked to increase the considerable fortune he inherited from his father. Peter and I had been trying for months to get him to put this paper on its feet, but nothing would shift him. I told Peter right from the start that it was useless, but he wouldn't entirely give up hope until the other night."

"But how...?" began Beef.

Wakefield turned on him like a schoolmaster interrupted during an English literature lesson by a boy who wished to leave the room. "That night was our final attempt," said Wakefield, "and we had agreed that if he refused to help us then, we would give up hope of his assistance. It so happened that there had arrived that day in the office a book for review which we knew would please him, and Peter had decided to take it down. Stewart was not, you will observe, the kind of man with whom any particular subtlety was needed. The book was one of those ghastly great illustrated editions of the Rubáiyát of Omar Khayyám, which, one had hoped, had passed out of popularity long ago. It was quarto in size, bound in white buckram with a grotesque display of ornamental gilt lettering on the sides and back. It was printed on hand-made paper, and its coloured plates were by some woman who had a passion for purples and pinks. Stewart liked to read aloud quotations from this overrated poem, and it was part of Peter's ingenuous plan that we should ask him to do so that evening.

"We reached the house at a quarter to eight, and Benson arrived about five minutes later. He was a florid, race-going sort of fellow, essentially provincial, and rather a bore. I could see no particular reason why anyone should wish to murder him, any more than one would have thought they wished to murder all members of his type. He mentioned that his car was out of order and that his wife wasn't well—the sort of conversation that one would expect from him. After dinner in the library we actually allowed Stewart to read several passages. Then we came to the point. Would he, or would he not, buy enough shares in the *Passing Moment* to keep it alive? He would not. Peter wasted a certain amount of valuable time in trying to make him change his mind, then we got up to go. Duncan arrived, apparently from nowhere, with our coats, Peter started up that old bus of his, and we came back to London. He dropped me at my flat and drove away. There you have the whole thing, and unless there are any questions you feel you must ask, I won't take any more of your time."

Beef stood up straight away. "No," he said, "there's no questions about the dinner-party. You've told me all I want to know. But," he added, stepping almost threateningly towards Wakefield, "there's one thing I want to hear from you. What did you do after Peter Ferrers left you at your rooms?"

"I thought that was coming," smiled Wakefield. "As it happens, I went straight to bed."

"And I," said Beef, "thought *that* was coming. Good morning, Mr. Wakefield." And with an air of conscious triumph, he stalked out of the office, leaving Wakefield and me to exchange glances; his of comprehension, mine of apology.

Chapter VII

ON the drive down to Sydenham I asked Beef about the whisky he had persuaded me to appropriate from the Cypresses. "You told me you'd explain it, Beef," I said, glancing mischievously at the figure beside me, for I was convinced that he had taken it for quite unprofessional reasons.

"So I will, in due time," he said. "That's got to be analysed."

"Analysed?" I repeated, smiling at this gross piece of subterfuge. "Why should you want the whisky analysed when the man's been stabbed?"

"Because," returned Beef quite seriously, "I believe it contained arsenic." And that was all he would say.

The girl Rose opened the door at the Cypresses, and showed us again into the library, where we found Peter alone. He looked unhappy and tired, I thought, though he said good morning, and offered us cigarettes. "The police have been here again this morning," he said. "There seems to be no doubt at all that poor old Duncan committed suicide."

"I'm very sorry about it, sir," said Beef, and there seemed to be genuine sympathy in his voice. "Must be very upsetting for you, having known him all your life."

Peter nodded. "Yes," he said, "we all feel it. He was as loyal a man as you could want to meet. And although in this last year or two he seemed to have become nervy, and highly strung, he always did his job rather better than one could expect. I was fond of him in an odd way. I can remember him taking me to kindergarten, and coming to meet me afterwards."

"But have you any idea what made him do it?" blundered Beef.

"I rather think it was the strain of all this business. I know he felt very worried at the thought that he might be called up to give evidence, and that his evidence might tell against my brother. However, his wife will be able to tell you more than I can. Would you like me to call her?"

"Perhaps it would be as well," said Beef.

Mrs. Duncan was as short and stalwart as her husband had been narrow and pale. Her arms seemed to be bursting out of her dress, and her face was large and white like a plain suet pudding. She showed no signs of grief at her recent loss, but her expression was resentful. And one felt at once that she had mastered the nervous Duncan as easily as she ruled the rest of the kitchen. There was something a little unhealthy about her, the faint odour of perspiration perhaps, or the heavy fleshiness of her figure.

"Very sorry to hear of your loss," said Beef ponderously.

"Mm," returned Mrs. Duncan, as though she were dubiously accepting a tribute.

"You have no doubt in your mind that he committed suicide?" asked Beef.

"Oh no," said the cook. "He'd threatened to do it a dozen times. He was so upset with all this." She glanced accusingly at Peter Ferrers. "And it's hardly a wonder."

"Still," said Beef complacently, "one would have thought it would take more than a to-do of this kind to make a normal man do himself in. If he'd handled as many murders as I have, he'd have known better."

"It wasn't the murder," said Mrs. Duncan, "it was his attachment to the family. I always told him he thought too much about his work. He couldn't sleep at night if everything wasn't just right. 'Do your job and have done with it,' I used to say. But no, he'd be wondering if Mr. Stewart had liked this, and fidgeting over Mr. Peter saying that, until he was little better than a ninny. And then when this happened he was nearly off his head. I told him straight that I didn't see that Benson was much loss. But all he'd say was, 'If you knew all that I know,' or, 'I hope I never have to tell all I can tell,' or something of that sort."

"There you are," said Beef triumphantly to Peter and me, "I told you yesterday he knew more than he'd say."

"Well, if he did," argued his widow, "he's took it with him to his grave, for he never told me nothing.

He'd worry and fidget and jump as though someone had come up behind him, and mumble in his sleep, but he never give nothing away."

"When did you notice his manner changing?" asked Beef.

"Well, he's never really been the same since the old gentleman died. Though you'd think that the bit of money he came into would have cheered him up."

"How much was it?" asked Beef, and I felt that his question was prompted by the merest curiosity.

"Oh, not a great lot," said Mrs. Duncan guardedly. "Three hundred pounds, or thereabouts. With what he had saved up it would have been enough to buy a nice little pub somewhere. Only, of course, he wouldn't listen to that. He had to be hanging round here looking after Mr. Stewart for the rest of his days; and this is what's come of it!"

"Still," said Beef consolingly, "perhaps you'll be able to have a house yourself now."

"I've every intention," said Mrs. Duncan, "as soon as this blows over."

"Would you mind telling me what your husband said that makes you so certain that he did commit suicide?"

"Well, he *said* he was going to do himself in," said Mrs. Duncan. "He told me so last night. It was after you'd been questioning him again. It was bad enough having to answer all the police asked him, without you coming along. He said, 'I can't face the court.' It nearly drove him off his head having to attend the coroner's. And then knowing that there would be Mr. Stewart's trial as well, it was too much for him. Besides, he left a note."

"He left a note, did he?"

"Yes, on the kitchen table. The police have took it now, though it was meant for me. Said he couldn't stand no more of it; questioning and that; and was going to hang himself. And that's what he did do. In my scullery too, and only wearing his nightshirt."

"What time would that have been?"

"I couldn't say, I'm sure. He came up to bed the same time as I did last night—round about ten. 'Course, we ought never to have stayed in this house after the murder. But we were told we should be wanted to give evidence, so what could we do? I think it turned poor Duncan's head, being in and out of the library where they found the corpse. Anyway, there he was in the morning."

"You both slept in the same room, then?" queried Beef.

"Yes," admitted Mrs. Duncan shortly.

"Separate beds?" Beef suggested.

"If you must go into such details, yes," he was told.

"But you never heard him get up and go out?"

"No. But there'd be nothing unusual in that. He was very restless at night, very restless."

Beef's voice grew sepulchral. "And where is he now?" he asked the cook.

She seemed the least embarrassed person. "In

the scullery with a sheet over him. The police have seen to him."

Beef recrossed his legs. "Now I want to ask you a few questions about the past," he said.

Mrs. Duncan became guarded in her manner. "There's not much I can tell you," she assured him.

"For instance, what regular visitors was there at the house?"

"Very few, really," she said. "There was the Reverend Smyke used to come round when he wanted a subscription to something, and Doctor Benson, and of course Mr. Peter, and really I can't remember anyone else who came more than once."

"What about when old Mr. Ferrers was alive?"

"It was just the same, very few strangers. There was his lawyer, a Mr. Nicholson, and another gentleman like a lawyer that was often in and out, but I think he came to see Mr. Stewart."

"What was his name?" asked Beef, busy with his notebook.

"Orpen, I think it was," returned the cook as though she grudged the information.

"Do you remember him?" asked Beef, turning to Peter Ferrers.

"Yes, I remember him quite well. I believe his real name was Oppenstein. I never knew his business."

"Has he been lately?" Beef asked Mrs. Duncan.

"I think he came once just after old Mr. Ferrers died, but I've never seen him since."

"Hm. Well, I think that's all I want to know from

you, Mrs. Duncan. Thank you very much. Oh—by the way..."

She turned back from the doorway which she had already reached. "What is it now?" she asked.

"Who ran the housekeeping accounts?"

As far as it was possible for one of that build, she stiffened. "I did," she said loudly.

"Anyone go over them?"

"I don't know whether Mr. Stewart did or didn't, and it wouldn't have made any difference if he had," she said in a breath. "I handed my book in at the end of the month and it was all correct. I paid the girls their wages, and Duncan and me ours. Bought all the insurance stamps and had charge of everything. And if there's anything you'd like to call into question..."

"Oh no," said Beef, "I'm sure it's all down."

After which it was no wonder that Mrs. Duncan slammed the door as she went out.

Beef turned to Peter Ferrers. "Can't hardly wonder at the old chap hanging himself when he'd got tied up to that, can you?" he said. Then, seeming to recollect that for Peter it was not a facetious matter of following clues and being entertained, but a tragedy in which two old friends had already lost their lives, and his brother was being held for murder, he added vaguely, "All the same, I'm sorry about it."

Peter nodded. "Yes, she is rather much, isn't she?" he said. "Still, she's a good cook."

"Did the police say they'd be back?" asked Beef.

Peter glanced at his wrist-watch. "Yes, at about midday, they said."

"Who was in charge?" asked Beef inquisitively.

"There was an Inspector Stute."

Beef slapped his thigh with a large hand. "Cor, ole Stute," he grinned. "I wonder what he'll say when he finds me down here. I'm afraid he never thought much of me, didn't Stute. He was always on about his modern methods and that, and didn't like the way I went straight to the heart of a thing."

I looked at Beef with some concern. In the old days he had at least the grace to be modest about himself when he was in contact with more intelligent detectives. But his having set up as a private investigator seemed to have turned his head. Even at this minute his professional air was very obvious as he asked Peter where the nearest telephone was.

The Cypresses was not on the telephone, but there was a call-box apparently a few yards down the road. When Beef and I reached it he insisted rather childishly that I should squeeze myself into the box with him while he made his call. In the restricted space he began to search through the directory.

"Hm," he said at last, "only three Oppensteins. That's good."

His big blunt finger seemed to have some difficulty with the work of dialling, but eventually he got through. I listened while, with elephantine attempts at tact, he asked someone at the other end if he knew Mr. Ferrers, and received, I gathered, a curt negative. Undaunted, he dialled again, and this time got as far as saying, "Oh, you did know him, then?" before the other refused to discuss his business, or so I gathered. Beef's face was lively as he put down the receiver and looked round at me.

"I thought so," he said, "a moneylender, that's what he was."

Chapter VIII

W HEN the front-door bell rang, Ferrers remarked quietly that it was probably the police, and he was right. And in a few minutes Inspector Stute was ushered into the room by Rose. I had not seen him since we had met over the Braxham case, and was a little apprehensive about his attitude to Beef. I remembered his dapper appearance, and cool, efficient manner, and I knew that in this case, at all events, he would have little patience with my blundering friend.

However, he nodded with curt friendliness to Beef. "I heard you were here," he said pleasantly. "You've set up on your own as a detective, then?"

"That's right," returned Beef, and I felt there was something aggressive in his manner. "And I've just come down here to get this little matter of Mr. Stewart Ferrers cleared up. I already know enough to be sure he ought never to have been arrested."

Stute nodded, smiling. "That's right, Beef," he said, "you go ahead."

"Only," said Beef, "I think it would save a lot of time and trouble for all parties if you was to tell me on what you base your case against Stewart Ferrers."

Still Stute remained unruffled. "Oh, you do," he said. "Well now. Look here. You run along like a good chap and don't take up our time. I'm pleased to see you again, but really, this sort of thing is too urgent for me to be delayed by anyone."

Peter Ferrers suddenly stood up. "Well, I think I'll leave you two to discuss the matter between yourselves," he said. "I have no wish to hear the whole case over again." And he walked out of the room.

Beef had been sucking gently at the ends of his moustache. Then, "That's not hardly fair, Inspector Stute," he burst out as soon as Peter Ferrers had left the room. "You know very well what's always done in these cases. You tell me what you know, and I tell you what I know, and we're all Sir Garnet."

Stute sighed. "Well, very briefly I'll outline to you the case," he said. "It's so clear that anyone who's even read the newspapers probably understands it. Only, I would ask you, Beef, not to start a lot of discussion afterwards. You really mustn't presume on the luck you had in that other matter to take up time elsewhere. First of all, and most important, Stewart's finger-prints were quite clearly on the handle of the dagger with which Benson was murdered, and no other finger-prints were on it. Then again, Stewart had quarrelled with Benson that evening, as we found out from Duncan, and their quarrel had been a serious one. Stewart was alone in the house with Benson, except for the servants, at the time of the murder. The butler, the cook, and the two housemaids can surely be left out of suspicion for lack of motive, or even capacity.

"Then there is the evidence of the chauffeur-gardener. Stewart most carefully gave him the evening off, but he also cross-examined him on the subject of pre-selection gears, knowing that Benson's car had these. His idea was to drive Benson away in his own car and let him be found, having apparently committed suicide, in some place from which he himself could walk home. Then again, we have a document which you haven't seen yet. I don't really know why I should show it to you, but since it will probably convince you once and for all that you're wasting my time in hanging around here, here it is. This, I may say, was found in Stewart's pocket when he was arrested."

He pulled out of his pocket a piece of folded paper about eight inches by four, on which had been typewritten these remarkable words:

"Received of St. Vincent Ferrer, forty seven years of hellish life now to be ended, with a total profit of £500."

There was a twopenny stamp below this across which was the signature of Benson.

"Now," said Stute, "our handwriting experts have made a thorough examination of this document, and they say that the signature is the genuine signature of Benson. What is the inference? It is perfectly obvious. This was a document prepared for Benson to sign under the impression that he was signing a receipt for five hundred pounds, but actually serving as a preadmission of suicide. Having refilled Benson's glass with whisky a number of times, and having paid him the money, Stewart handed him the receipt to sign, and Benson had no idea that he was signing his own death warrant.

"Stewart's idea, then, had been to put Benson in his own car and drive away to some lonely spot where he would leave him with the dagger in his throat, his hand on the dagger, and the document showing that he intended to commit suicide in his pocket. But this is where the hitch came; the hitch which fortunately always comes to make the detection of murderers possible. *Benson hadn't brought his car*. What was Stewart to do? Either drive him away in his own, and involve himself in a hundred ways; blood on his cushions, the fact that he'd taken his car out at all, and the possibility of his being seen? No, he could not do that. Finally, he decided to leave him there in the chair. After all, nobody had seen him commit the murder, and he didn't see how it could be proved against him.

"But it can. For me it would need no more than a process of elimination to be sure that it was Stewart. It was someone *in* the house. It wasn't one of the servants, and Stewart had both the strength and the motive to do it. But as you have seen, my case doesn't rest on that."

"Is that your case?" asked Beef.

Again Stute smiled with long-suffering good-humour. "There's a lot more to it," he said. "I've discovered the motive for one thing—or perhaps even the motives. No one who has been in Sydenham since this murder happened could possibly be in doubt about one thing—the relationship between Stewart and Mrs. Benson. There was nobody in the place who had not heard stories about it, and it is possible that Benson's murder was no more than the outcome of the eternal triangle."

"But what about the five hundred pounds?"

"I've been to see Stewart's bank and it appears that he has drawn out altogether four sums of five hundred in single pound notes in the last two years. What could that be but blackmail? When Benson showed himself ready to sign a receipt for five hundred pounds, what, one must ask, was he receiving five hundred pounds for? Scarcely professional services. That, surely, is sufficient, though I daresay we shall find some more details between now and the date of the trial."

"But, then," persisted Beef, "if he'd handed that money over to Benson, and got a receipt for it, why wasn't it in Benson's pocket? Or was it?"

"It wasn't," said Stute, "but it was in Stewart's bedroom. We found it with the faked confession of suicide when we arrested him."

"There's a couple more questions I'd like to ask," Beef postulated.

"Certainly," said Stute.

"Did you find any foot-prints round the drive or in the garden on the morning of the murder?"

Stute laughed aloud. "Come now, Beef," he said kindly. "You must try to keep up to date, you know. Foot-prints!"

"All right, all right," said Beef. "Only I know what I'm thinking," he added mysteriously.

"There's one other little point," Stute added. "You saw where the dagger was found? In its place on the table. Who would have put it there? Surely only one man. The man who kept it there, who played with it a dozen times a day and always returned it to the same spot. Circumstantial, I know, but very convincing.

"You see," he said finally, turning to me, "I know the position, Mr Townsend. The police always arrest the wrong man, and then the wonderful private detective comes along and shows them how mistaken they are. I'm sorry, I should have liked to see you make a good story of this, but this time it's not going your way. I'm afraid there can be no doubt whatever about it. Stewart is guilty, and we shan't have much difficulty in proving it. Next time you want to get the material for a mystery you'll really have to follow the Yard's investigations."

I sighed. What he had said was only too true.

But Beef was not impressed. "There are one or two 'oles I should like to pick in that," he said. "For instance, how did he come to be so silly as to have left the knife out on the table? I mean, why didn't he make any show of Benson having committed suicide? He never even had the confession of suicide in his pocket."

Stute smiled with patronizing ease. "You know, Beef, what's wrong with you is lack of experience. You get your murders out of books, where they're all brilliantly subtle, and concealed behind extra-ordinary evidence. Murder in real life is a straight-forward business, committed by some blundering fool. Instead of thinking of all the cases in these detective novels that Mr. Townsend believes in, why don't you study a few of those that appear in the papers? You'll find that murderers are not such extremely clever people, and what thinking they do is done later."

Beef seemed a little crestfallen, for he said no more.

At this point we were interrupted by the entrance of a breezy young doctor who at once told Stute that he had made his examination.

"What of?" broke in Beef.

There was a twinkle in Stute's eye as he turned to the doctor. "This is ex-Sergeant Beef," he said, "who is making a private investigation of the case for Mr. Peter Ferrers."

The doctor nodded a hurried greeting. "I've been examining the corpse of the butler," he said to Beef, and then turning to Stute, added, "There are no signs of violence at all. I don't think there can be the slightest doubt that he committed suicide without coercion."

"Thank you, doctor," said Stute, "that's all I wanted to know, and I was fairly certain of it. The poor old chap may even have witnessed the murder. Certainly he knew that his employer was guilty. The onus of this knowledge was too much for him—a normally honest man—and his way out, in the circumstances, is understandable. He had practically told his wife this, and though it's very distressing, I cannot feel surprised."

"Do you mind if I have a look at the corpse?" said Beef.

Stute became even more indulgent. "Well, if you like," he said. "Run down now, only don't waste time over it, because I've got to get back to the Yard. I can't think why you should want to see it, it's not a pleasant sight."

I shuddered as Beef walked out of the room. "It's the last thing I should want to do," I said.

"I'm afraid it's only curiosity," said Stute. "He was always a man never to 'miss anything.' Well, good morning, Townsend. I hope your old policeman provides you with some good situations. Come along, doctor." And the two walked smartly from the room.

When I remembered the puzzled Stute I had known at Braxham, energetically following up this and that, I noticed the contrast with this suave and confident detective. This time, as he had so pointedly said, there was no doubt.

Chapter IX

WHEN Beef came back into the room he was with Peter Ferrers. "Suicide all right," he said.

"The police had already established that," I said with some exasperation.

Beef ignored me. "Could I have a look at that book as you gave your brother that night?" he asked Peter.

I thought that perhaps there was a flicker of hesitation or embarrassment in Peter's glance as he heard this. But he said nothing as he went over to the table and picked up the elaborate edition of Omar Khayyám.

Beef turned the thick pages of the big volume slowly in his hands, and finally let go his most triumphant ejaculation. "Ah," he said, "I know which part he was reading to you."

I did what was expected of me. "How did you find that out?" I asked.

Beef looked up, his face lit with simple pleasure. "I seen which pages have been cut. See! There's only two! He couldn't have read very much."

"No," said Peter, "he didn't."

"What letters is these on the top?" he asked after a moment's thought.

I blushed for him. "Roman numerals," I explained in a whisper, for Peter was at the other end of the room. "That's verse sixty-four."

"Then he must have started here," said Beef, turning over the pages, "and he couldn't have read no further than that one."

"No," I said, "and that's verse seventy-one."

Beef began to read:

> *"Said one—'Folks of a surly Tapster tell,*
> *And daub his Visage with the Smoke of Hell;*
> *They talk of some strict Testing of us—Pish!*
> *He's a Good Fellow, and 'twill all be well.'*

Now I wonder why he was so keen on that one," he said when he had finished. "Sounds as though it might mean something."

"It does mean something," I hastened to put in, with some irritation and some irony.

"Oh, I know, I know," said Beef, "I'm not talking about the poetry. I mean it might have some 'inner significance' for someone what was in that room. I like this last one, though. This bit:

> *"I often wonder what the Vintners buy*
> *One half so precious as the Goods they sell.*

"Funny, I said that to myself a dozen times. Reminds me of the story of the man who bought a public-house, and when they asked him what time he was going to open, he said he wasn't going to open. He was going to drink the beer himself." And Beef gave his gross guffaw.

This was too much for Peter Ferrers. "Look here," he said, turning round, and for the first time showing real anger, "I don't think this is the place or the time for you to fool about."

Beef looked as guilty as a small boy caught in an orchard. The grin disappeared from his face, and he stood up. "Er—I'm very sorry, Mr. Ferrers," he said contritely. "I'm afraid I was forgetting myself for the minute."

It was perhaps lucky that the door burst open at this moment and one of the servant girls broke into the room.

"I've got something to tell," she said defiantly. "I didn't tell the police, either. But now Mr. Duncan is Gone, I think it only right you should hear."

All three of us examined the dumpy little figure that stood between us and the door. She was less than five feet tall, with a round, flat, innocent face and untidy reddish hair. In her somewhat soiled apron and blue print dress, her face flushed and her hands dirty, she looked the honest, blowzy, noisy wench that she probably was.

"Steady now, my girl, steady," said Beef, becoming dignified again. "Just you tell us quietly what you know, and you'll be all right."

The last phrase displeased her. "Oh, I know I shall be all right," she said briskly. "I'm only telling you because I think it's my duty."

Her story followed, told between gasps and asides with which she gave us to understand that she had suffered violently in her imagination from what she had seen, both at the time, and since then. She had been the first to go up to bed on the night of the murder, and, not expecting Rose to be late, had left the landing light on. In answer to a question from Beef as to whether Rose was often late she became clumsily coy and said surely Beef knew about Rose and Ed Wilson. Beef pretended that this was no surprise to him, made a note, and the girl Freda continued.

She must have dropped straight off to sleep, for she hadn't heard Rose come up, nor the cook, nor the butler. She had in fact heard nothing, until she had found herself wide awake in the darkness. She knew something must have woken her and she was rather frightened and thought of calling Rose in the next room. But just then she heard the front-door bell. Whoever can that be, it appears she had thought to herself, and unwillingly got out of bed. It seemed that no one else had been aroused by the ringing, though she thought now that it must have been going on for some time to have awoken her. She could hear Mrs. Duncan snoring, and no sound of movement on the servants' landing.

When Beef asked her what time it had been when she got out of bed she said she was certain she was not sure, and even when pressed to give some rough estimate she only insisted that she could not say.

Going on with her story, she said that she had pulled on her overcoat (she mentioned that she could not afford a dressing-gown) and began to go downstairs. But when she reached the first-floor landing she thought she'd have a look out of the window which commanded the drive to the front door. And as she did so she saw a man get on a bicycle and start up towards the front gate. But when he had nearly reached it he jumped off and turned back. There had been bright moonlight, she said, and she could see his outline distinctly. She hadn't recognized him, and she wouldn't recognize him again. He was black, standing there. We knew how people looked in the moonlight, she said. She hadn't been able to make out why he should have stopped and looked back, and was just beginning to wonder whether he had seen her, when she heard him call out, "Who's that down there?" sharply, as though he were frightened. He must have stood there, she thought, for two minutes, then suddenly he jumped on his bicycle and pedalled away.

She herself had not been able to move. She was, she now explained, glued to the spot. Her heart was going in a manner which she described as "fit to burst," while at the same time, and rather confusingly, she didn't know whether she was standing on her head or her heels. A feather, she assured us, would have been sufficient to send her prostrate. But it was fortunate that these metaphors, however mixed, had come into play, for they kept her there to see something else. A long time passed, she assured us, and then, as sure as she was standing before us now, a man emerged from the shrubbery near the front door. At this point Beef interrupted her.

"There!" he said. "I asked them if there was any foot-prints!"

This lonely and silent pedestrian had, the girl thought, kept to the grass borders at the edge of the drive, for although the night was so still that she had been enabled to hear her own respiration, she didn't catch the sound of his footsteps. No, she hadn't been able to recognize him. You couldn't see any face. All you could see was the shape of a man walking away.

It appeared that her information was exhausted, but, with the willingness of her type to oblige as much as possible, she was about to repeat it from the beginning. And when Peter Ferrers had told her kindly that that would do, she said, with a broad smile, that she hoped that she had been useful.

"Useful," growled Beef. "I don't know about that. It makes things two or three times more complicated. Still, I suppose you meant to do right," he added grandly. "You may go now."

Chapter X

PETER FERRERS asked us if we would have some lunch, but Beef declined, and as we were walking down the drive together he explained his refusal. "I noticed a nice little House down at the corner," he said, "where I shouldn't be surprised if we was to pick up some information."

I thought what an old hypocrite he was, but said nothing and resigned myself to the inevitable bread and cheese which was all the pub was likely to supply.

When we entered the Sheepdippers' Arms it seemed doubtful if we should get even that. What Beef had called a "nice little house" turned out to be a small and dreary pub with the smell of last week's beer still hanging on the air in the taproom. There was no fire lit in the grate, and even the dart-board was pierced and decayed until a player's score would have been more dependent on faith than on mathematics. The man behind the bar eyed us morosely, and grudgingly took our order.

"I'll try a pint of your bitter," announced Beef, as if the publican should be flattered at a connoisseur of his experience experimenting here. Beef seemed quite unaware of the publican's failure to show us any welcome, and said brightly, "It's a nice day, isn't it?"

The man scarcely nodded, and stood there with his face averted from us. An old lady over in the public bar called shrilly for another glass of ruby wine, and we noticed that the sourness in his manner was not for us alone, for he served her without a word.

"I wonder if you've got a nice piece of bread and cheese?" asked Beef when the publican had returned to our side of the bar.

"No, we don't *do* bread and cheese."

This time Beef did seem a little crushed. "Hardly what you'd call matey," he commented aside to me. And then his face lit up. "Come and sit over here," he said. "I've got something to ask you."

We moved to an uncomfortable bench across from the bar and stood our tankards on a table. "What was that bit?" whispered Beef.

"Bit?" I asked, wholly unable to understand.

"You know, in that poem."

"Oh yes. I know what you mean.

> *"Said one—'Folks of a surly Tapster tell,*
> *And daub his Visage with the Smoke of Hell;*
> *They talk of some strict Testing of us—Pish!*
> *He's a Good Fellow, and 'twill all be well.' "*

Beef nodded excitedly. "How do we know it's not him?" he said, indicating the man behind the bar.

"We don't," I returned curtly, "but we have absolutely no reason for thinking it is. Drink your beer and let's get back to the Cypresses."

But Beef wouldn't be hurried. And when a few

minutes later a young man in the overalls of a
motor-mechanic lounged in, he became embar-
rassingly talkative.

"Do you work round these parts?" he asked, with
a directness I should have thought the mechanic
would have resented.

"Yes, I've got a little garage of my own round the
corner."

"Oh, did you have anything to do with Benson's
car?" asked Beef.

" 'Course I did," said the mechanic cheerfully.
"In fact, I've wondered the police haven't been to
see me already."

"The police don't find out everything," said Beef
with a meaning glance at me. Whereupon he pulled
out of his pocket-case one of his newly printed cards.
"I'm investigating this case," he said, "on behalf
of Mr. Peter Ferrers, and if there's any information
you can give me, I shouldn't half be grateful."

The mechanic looked at him squarely and smiled.
I liked his frank and pleasant face, his lively
boyish eyes and obvious intelligence. "There's
quite a lot I can tell," he said, "though I don't know
whether it'll be any use to you. Mr. Wilkinson here
might be able to tell you something too." And he
indicated the publican.

"Why? How would he know anything?" asked
Beef.

"Used to be gardener up there," explained the
mechanic in a low voice. "The old man left him
enough money to buy the pub, but he still goes up

for a walk round to see how Wilson's getting on with the garden sometimes. I don't say he does know anything, but he might."

"Well, let's hear what you can tell us," said Beef. "Have a drink?"

The young man said he didn't mind, and began at once to tell us quite freely what details he could remember. He had heard, it seemed, the story of Stewart and Mrs. Benson, though he could never remember their having driven into his garage together. On the evening of the murder Benson had brought his car in on the way to the Cypresses for dinner. It was missing on one cylinder, he said, and he wanted him, Fred Coleman, to examine it and get it right. If he could have it running before about ten he was to bring it to the Cypresses. If not, Benson would have a taxi home and the car was to be delivered at his own house. It was absolutely essential, Dr. Benson had said, to have it ready for the morning when he had a round to make and several important visits.

Young Coleman had worked on the car for much longer than he had anticipated, and it must have been little short of midnight when he eventually got it going. He knew that it would be no good taking it to the Cypresses at that hour, since Dr. Benson would already have gone home. He didn't mind telling us that he cursed having to work so late on the car, but Benson was a good customer and he didn't like to disappoint him for his morning round of visits. So he drove off to Benson's house, which was a quarter of a mile away. He could see that the lights were still on in the downstairs windows when he got there, so he rang the front-door bell. The door was opened by Mrs. Benson.

He turned aside at this point of his narrative to inform us that he had always considered Mrs. Benson a smart piece of goods, to which Beef, I'm ashamed to say, gave an understanding "Ah." And when she came to the door that evening, wearing as he said, nothing but a pair of pyjamas and a bit of a dressing-gown pulled over them, it had given him quite a turn. And what she had told him had been most surprising. Benson was not yet home though he had promised not to be later than halfpast ten. She was very worried about him, as she knew he had a heavy day in front of him tomorrow.

She had not, however, as it appeared to young Coleman, looked particularly worried. He might be wrong, he admitted, but he had almost thought that she was on the point of asking him in. Then she had "grown serious" and begged him to drive back to the Cypresses and bring her husband home. The Cypresses, as Beef already knew, was not on the telephone, since Stewart had inherited his father's prejudice.

On his way down the engine had given out again and he had left it at his garage and gone on his bicycle to the Cypresses. He had found the place, so far as he could see, completely in darkness, and no sign of life anywhere in the grounds of the house. It had looked, he told us, very gloomy at that time of night, and when he had rung the bell and heard it pealing away somewhere in the house with no one taking any notice of it, he had been only too glad to get on his bicycle and cycle away.

Then came his other, more remarkable revelations. It was a bright moonlit night, and as he cycled down the drive, the shadows of the bushes were thrown in his path. He wouldn't be quite sure now, but he thought it was some change in the shape of these shadows which had made him turn his head, and he was almost certain that he had seen someone moving among the bushes behind him. He had got off his bicycle and waited a minute, shouting "Who's there?" or something of the sort. There had been no reply, and after a few minutes he had decided not to delay any further but to get to bed. He did, however, stop at his garage to telephone to Mrs. Benson. He told her that her husband must have left the Cypresses and be on his way home now. He explained that the engine of the car had given out again, and promised to set to work on it first thing in the morning.

Beef had only one question to ask. "Did anyone see you around the house that night?"

"Yes," returned young Coleman, "there was a policeman on the corner whom I know. I said good night to him as I went past."

"Well, thank you very much," said Beef, "your story fits in nicely."

"If you want to know anything else," Coleman

told us, "come round to the garage. Only I must get back there now as I've two or three repairs to do this afternoon. Here's the address. I'll be glad to give you any information I can." He nodded cheerfully and left the bar.

"It strikes me," I observed, "that that young mechanic may know more about the actual murder than he's going to admit. His story was very well put together, but don't forget he had to find some way of explaining why he was up at the Cypresses that evening after midnight, because the policeman saw him."

"I'm not forgetting anything," said Beef, and moved across to the bar.

But when he tried to draw the ex-gardener publican into conversation, he was most dismally unsuccessful.

Chapter XI

"Look here, Beef," I said, as we left the cheerless inn, "it's time we went to see Mrs. Benson."

"Why? Have you made an appointment with her?" asked Beef.

"No, I mean we need a woman in this case. It's getting too tied up with details and not enough human interest."

Beef chuckled. "All right," he said, "we'll go and see her if you feel like that about it, only I don't expect much from this, I don't mind telling you."

"She sounds attractive."

"Wait till you see her," said Beef. "You never want to go on other people's opinions. I've been terribly took in that way before now. Have you got the address?"

I had, and I told it to him. "But don't, for goodness' sake, forget," I added, "that we are going to see a widow. It won't be the occasion for any of your attempted jokes. And do try to be polite."

Beef only grunted, and we started to climb the hill towards Benson's house. It was a long and tiring walk through the respectable but gloomy streets of Sydenham, and when at last we stood at the front door of Benson's fair-sized, semi-detached house, most of my enthusiasm for this interview had been damped. Beef pushed the electric bell, holding his thumb on the button far longer than he should have done. But the door was not opened.

"Funny," said Beef, and before I could restrain him he had rung again. This time I thought there was some faint sound from the back, but it was not until after Beef's third and most nerve-wracking ring that we could distinctly hear footsteps in the passage, and at last saw the door pulled open.

Sheila Benson wore a dressing-gown. What she had on under it is a subject for discussion between Beef and myself to this day. I'm not going to tell you my theory on this subject, or Beef's crude conclusions, but I must confess that whenever the subject occurs, the Sergeant is apt to guffaw and nudge me painfully and rudely in the ribs.

She certainly was handsome. She was neither pretty nor beautiful, but she had one of those attractive, changeful faces, with biggish lips that smiled very often and quite disarmingly, with a golden warm complexion, dark brilliant eyes, and a frank, unsuppressed vitality.

Beef seemed rather taken aback by this apparition. "I *had* come to ask some questions," he stuttered.

His reward was a smile. "Why, you must be Sergeant Beef," said Mrs. Benson; "Peter has told me all about *you*. Come in, won't you?"

Still Beef hesitated. "If I've come at an inconvenient moment," he began.

"Inconvenient? Not at all," said Sheila Benson.

"I've been gardening."

Realizing that this was just what the story needed, I gave Beef a surreptitious shove, and he stumbled into the hall.

"Come in, won't you?" said Mrs. Benson. "This is the old waiting-room. The rest of the house is a bit untidy. I haven't had a servant since the upset."

"You mean," said Beef sepulchrally, "since your husband was murdered?"

"That's it," said Mrs. Benson, without dropping her bright manner.

"If I may say so, madam," Beef went on, "you don't seem to be very put out by your loss."

"What makes you think that?" asked Mrs. Benson in the tone of one who genuinely seeks information.

Beef coughed, and was at a loss for a moment, while I wondered how he would extricate himself from the embarrassment into which his own clumsiness had brought him.

"Well, I mean," he mumbled, "you're not wearing mourning, are you?"

Mrs. Benson smiled. "I'm not wearing anything much, am I?" she said. "What about some tea?"

Beef was relieved. "I could do with a cup of tea," he said faintly.

"I'll have to make it myself. You two just sit there and wait," and she gaily swished from the room.

Beef pulled out a handkerchief and mopped his forehead. "What do you say to that?" he asked in an awed voice.

"She's certainly rather overwhelming," I admitted.

"A woman who could behave like that just after her lawful husband had been stabbed to death might do anything," Beef announced, and after a moment added, "Anything."

When Sheila Benson returned with the tea she was wearing a plain frock, and she had evidently combed her hair.

"Sugar?" she asked Beef. "And what have you come to find out from *me*, I wonder?"

Beef sipped noisily from a teacup which he grasped with both hands. "Was you in love with Stewart Ferrers?" he asked explosively, as he put it down empty.

Sheila Benson had a surprise for both of us. "Good Lord, no," she said, "I'm in love with Peter. Have been for a year or more."

Beef gasped. "He never told us," he blurted out.

"Well," said Sheila Benson, "men are rather reserved in these matters. It's not everyone who would speak as frankly as I do."

"No," admitted Beef, "it certainly isn't. Did your husband know about this?"

"Oh yes, he'd known for a long time," said Sheila Benson. "It didn't worry him. He wasn't the man to worry over that sort of thing. Now if he lost a lot of money racing, he *did* get annoyed."

Suddenly, to my horror, Beef put his teacup down and began what I can only describe as a tirade.

"I suppose this is what is called modern morality," he announced. "Stories going round the place about you and one brother and all the time you're carrying on with the other. Then your husband gets murdered and you don't seem to care a straw. I quite believe what that young mechanic said about you giving him a come-hither look. I'm thankful I didn't arrive here alone myself this afternoon. I don't know what people are coming to I'm sure. In a respectable place like Sydenham, too. I never expect anyone to be churchy all the time, but I do think you might take it seriously when your husband gets his throat cut. It's not hardly decent. I'm a good mind to throw up the case immediately."

Sheila Benson smiled. "Oh, don't do that, Sergeant," she said, "just when you and I were getting on so well."

Beef seemed slightly, but unwillingly, mollified. "How do you mean, your husband didn't mind?" he persisted.

"My husband, whatever his faults, was a man of some experience," explained Sheila Benson. "He drank too much, he neglected his work, he was a bully, and I daresay worse things as well, but he wasn't narrow-minded. He saw that Peter and I were in love, and he was quite willing that we should arrange matters in some way. He himself would have preferred, I think, for his own purposes, to be without a wife at home. And he certainly couldn't have expected me to sit at home waiting for him after some of his behaviour."

"I see," said Beef. "He was a bit of a dog himself, was he?"

"Too apt," replied Sheila Benson, "if you knew this district."

"Then," said Beef, his manner suddenly brightening as he seized a welcome idea, "you don't believe in this quarrel between your husband and Stewart Ferrers over you?"

"Certainly not," said Sheila Benson. "I've told you before, there never was anything between Stewart and me. If they quarrelled it was over something else."

"But your name was mentioned," said Beef.

"I daresay, but I don't believe it could have been more than casually."

"Could it," asked Beef, "have caused a quarrel between Benson and Peter Ferrers?"

Sheila Benson smiled again. "No, not that either. They both understood the position too well, as I have told you. In fact, only that evening I had been talking it over with my husband."

Out came Beef's notebook. "Oh, you had?" he said, "and what did he say?"

"He said he'd have a chat with Peter about it, and see what could be arranged."

"Very nice indeed," returned Beef sarcastically. "You might have been talking over a picnic you was going to have."

"Well, I don't think any of us saw any reason to get excited," explained Sheila Benson. "Life's too short for hysteria."

"And did they have that little chat?" asked Beef.

"No, they never had a chance. Peter brought his

friend Wakefield that evening, a man I rather dislike, and Stewart was there the whole time."

"What did you think, then, when he didn't come home?"

Sheila Benson laughed outright. "If I had had to think of some explanation every time my husband was late during the years of our marriage, I should have been a lady novelist by now," she retorted. "I was only a little puzzled after I knew from young Coleman that he hadn't got the car with him."

"You stayed up for him, though?" said Beef.

At this she smiled ingratiatingly. "Well, I was reading Mr. Townsend's latest book about you, Sergeant," she said, "and was far too interested to think of bed."

I could see that Beef was delighted though he did his best to hide it. "I'm glad that someone reads it, even if it's only someone in my new case," was his involved reply. "What time did you go to bed?"

"I really don't know. It must have been about an hour after Coleman called."

"So you didn't know till next morning that he hadn't been in all night?"

"No. As a matter of fact, I didn't know until the police rang up and told me. We haven't shared a room for ages," she added.

"Oh, I see. Has your husband ever had anything to do with the police before?" he asked in tones of some suspicion.

"Only when we had a burglary a couple of years ago," said Sheila Benson in a rather bored voice.

"That was a silly affair which came through his not locking the surgery window properly. They didn't get into the house, though, so there was nothing to claim from the insurance. But. . ."

Beef interrupted her. "You know I meant anything on the *wrong* side of the police," he put in tersely.

"Oh, I see what you mean. Well, nothing that I know of—though I'd never be surprised with my late husband."

Beef nodded. "No more shouldn't I," he agreed. "Well, I think that's all the information I'll ask you for at present," and he stood up.

"Would you like to see my garden before you go?" asked Sheila Benson sweetly.

"I think that's a pleasure I'll postpone," said Beef grandly. "In the circumstances I must return to my duties," and he picked up his hat to leave the house.

Chapter XII

THAT evening, when I had driven Beef back to Lilac Crescent, I dined alone and decided to spend an hour in my own study working on the case. After all, I argued to myself, if Beef could find a solution, there was no reason why I shouldn't. I had as much experience as he had of murder mysteries, and, I flattered myself, rather more intelligence.

I decided to make a list of the points first, and then of people, and see what sort of sense emerged from them. We had discovered a great deal in our investigations which, so far as we knew, the police knew nothing about. And it was out of this material that a solution must come if Stewart were not guilty. So I wrote:

1. *Omar Khayyám.*

Beef had taken tremendous interest in this book, and he at least felt, I guessed, that it had some bearing on the case. It was surely not a coincidence that it had been given to Stewart on the night of the murder. While a reading from it as entertainment for bachelor guests at the dinner was sufficiently extraordinary to make one wonder if it had not been used as some form of communication. Could it be possible, as Beef had suggested, that the "surly Tapster" referred to Wilkinson, the ex-gardener publican? The verse had gone on to talk of his visage being smeared by the smoke of Hell. Did this mean that somebody had suggested that he was a villain? And when in the last line, the poem said "He's a Good Fellow, and 'twill all be well," did this mean that the supposition was mistaken, or that he had been bribed or persuaded into something which would save somebody's plans from interference by him? It was a little fantastic perhaps, but not altogether impossible.

2. *Bloodstains.*

Once before, I remembered, Beef had solved a murder mystery purely by noting the nature and position of bloodstains. He had kept very quiet this time about that mysterious extra bloodstain on the cushion. The knife, as it lay on the library table, was stained with blood, yet it had apparently been wiped on the cushion cover. What could this mean? Had the murderer plunged it into Benson's neck, withdrawn it, wiped it, and then inserted it again? It was a gruesome thought and seemed to lead nowhere. Yet, as Beef had often remarked, everything means something, and you couldn't ignore a point like that.

3. *Poison.*

What had Beef meant by sniffing at the whisky and then suggesting that there had been arsenic in it? It seemed ludicrous to me that when a man had been stabbed to death, one should begin to talk about poison. Yet if that whisky had been doped there must be some explanation for it.

4. *Sheila-Stewart rumour.*

This was everywhere, yet so far we had found no confirmation of it. Everyone had bracketed the names of Sheila Benson and Stewart Ferrers, but no one whom we had questioned had actually seen them together. And when the murder had been mentioned to Sheila, she had calmly said it was Peter she loved, not Stewart. Was she lying now, or had the rumour lied? She had struck me as a flagrant and vulgar person, but not, I somehow felt, a liar. Could a rumour like this have gone through the whole district without some real foundation?

5. *The receipt.*

This was a most extraordinary document. Stute's explanation of it as a piece of nonsense so worded that it might be signed by a tipsy or a careless man in the belief that it was a receipt for £500 whereas it really represented the last words written by a man about to commit suicide, was a feasible one. But the wording was extremely odd. I looked along my reference shelf for some book which would tell me about the Saint mentioned in it, and finding the thick volume of Lippincott's *Dictionary of Biography*, I turned up "Ferrer" and found this entry:

"Ferrer (Vincenzo), in Latin, Vicentius Ferrerius, known as St. Vincent Ferrer, a Spanish Dominican, born at Valencia, January 23, 1357. He published a *Tractatus de Moderno Ecclesiae Schismate*, and was famous throughout Christendom for his miracles, his preaching, and his success in converting Jews and Saracens. Died at Vannes, in France, April 5, 1419."

Was I not reasonable in supposing that the name of a fourteenth-century Spanish Dominican, who had afterwards been canonized, had only been dragged into this because of its similarity to that of the two brothers? Or could the Saint have some actual influence in the matter? At all events there was a flimsy aspect of the police's explanation. If Stewart meant to stab the doctor, it was very hard to see how he was going to make anyone think that Benson had committed suicide. A doctor of all people would be the last to kill himself by that difficult and chancy means.

6. *Pre-selection gears.*

Was Stute right in attaching quite the importance he did to these simple inquiries from Stewart to Ed Wilson? It is true that the doctor's car had them, and that anybody who intended to drive such a car for the first time might well make a few inquiries about their working. But then so had hundreds of other cars pre-selection gears, and for all we knew Stewart might have thought of buying one. It was only as the words of a guilty man that his inquiries had any significance at all.

7. *The quarrel.*

The truth about this we should never know since Duncan had committed suicide, but it remained a significant, and a very important matter. Duncan had gathered that their quarrel was to do with Sheila, and yet Sheila herself had blandly stated that this was impossible as Benson was indifferent to her infidelities except as a possible means of freeing himself from the ties of married life. In any case, if she was to be believed, there had been no grounds for such a quarrel since her love-affair had been with Peter and not with Stewart. Over what then had they quarrelled that evening? Was it true that Benson was blackmailing Stewart? If so, on what grounds? What could he know about this quiet, church-going man, who seemed to be respected, if not particularly liked, in the district? Perhaps we should know something of that when we came to interview Stewart, but at present that quarrel seemed a misfit. As for the other sentence Duncan had heard, "It's in my surgery now," this might mean anything or nothing. It might be a casual reference to something Benson had borrowed

from Stewart, it might be one of a hundred trivial
details. On the other hand it might possibly refer to
some evidence of something through which he was
obtaining money from the elder brother.

8. *Money.*

I always looked for money considerations in such
crimes as these, and there were several here. First of all
there were the four sums of £500 each which had been
drawn by Stewart in £1 notes from his bank since he had
inherited his fortune. Large sums in small notes always
suggested blackmail. And one of these had been found
in a brown-paper parcel in Stewart's dressing-table
upstairs. It was, of course, possible to admit the police
theory that these had been drawn for, and possibly paid
to, Benson, and recovered from his body after the
murder. But apart from the inadvisability of admitting
any police theories, I had serious doubt on this score.
Then also on the subject of money there had been the
visitor to Stewart in his father's time; Mr. Orpen, alias
Oppenstein, who had turned out to be a money-lender.
How, if at all, did he come into the case? Could there be
any connection between him and St. Vincent Ferrer,
who was famous for his conversion of Jews?

9. *The dagger.*

This was, perhaps, the most puzzling clue of all. Why
had it been returned to the table when it might well have
been left in Benson's throat? Was one to admit Stute's
suggestion that it had been placed there by force of
habit by Stewart, who was its chief user? It had his
finger-prints on it, and yet it had been cleaned by Rose
after Stewart had left the house that day, and he had not
returned to the library till he had gone there with his
guests after dinner. It was, of course, the most damning
piece of evidence that Stute had.

10. *Figures in the drive.*

The girl Freda's evidence of having seen these two men was the most sensational, and probably the most significant, clue on which we had stumbled. Her story tallied with that of the young mechanic, and it was fairly safe to assume that the first man, the one with the bicycle, the one who had twice rung the front-door bell, was the mechanic himself. But what about that second man whose presence had so startled the first, and who had waited until the cyclist's disappearance before he had quietly crept away? Was he the murderer? That seemed a most important point on which we had still to decide.

11. *Front-door keys.*

So far as our information went, the only people with keys were Stewart, Duncan, Mrs. Duncan, Ed Wilson, Rose, and Freda. Now, since the house had been carefully locked up and no one had broken in, the murderer had to be one of the three following: (*a*) one of those with a key, mentioned above, (*b*) someone who secretly had a key and had not ever used it to the knowledge of those we had cross-examined, and (*c*) someone who had remained hidden in the house while Duncan had locked up. I noted down this point, but I realized that it still left the net a wide one.

12. *The "Passing Moment."*

Peter and Wakefield had badly wanted money for this, and Wakefield at least had seemed to me a man who would stop at nothing in attaining his means. Had they done more than ask Stewart for the money and resign themselves to his emphatic refusal?

This was all the evidence that I knew of which

had come to light, and I proceeded to consider the people so far involved in the case.

When I began to consider these I was faced by one very obvious difficulty. It was to divide them into those who might possibly have committed the murder, and those who couldn't have done so. In all the cases with which I had been connected this had been the first measure in finding suspects. What made it difficult now is that really only one of these people seemed to have any motive at all— and that was Stewart. With an absence of motive to guide one, one could go on listing possible murderers among people known and unknown, *ad infinitum*. One could start with the probables, those in and out of the house, and continue down to the individuals like the policeman who had been on duty that night, and further, to that half of the people in London who could not account for their movements at the time of Benson's murder.

So, instead of attempting to make a list of suspects, I decided to put down on paper the names of those who seemed to have some direct connection with the matter, and consider what we knew of them. This was my list:

1. *Stewart Ferrers*. We had not yet interviewed him, of course, though I understood that Peter was arranging with his solicitor for Beef to see him. (There seemed to me, by the way, something almost superstitious in Peter's faith in Beef. Only superstition could account for the trouble he was taking to give Beef every facility.)

But in the meantime, the personality of Stewart, so far as it had been revealed, was not very attractive. We had been taught to imagine him as a stern, uncharitable, religious man, keeping his own counsel, and his own bank balance. He had certainly been drawing these curious sums of money, and there seemed a good chance of his having been blackmailed. The actual circumstances of the crime as the police knew them were strongly against him, and it would need some startling work on Beef's part to exonerate him.

2. *Peter Ferrers*. He was a strong possibility, I had felt from the beginning, as a murderer. We hadn't yet investigated his alibi, but so far as we knew there was no reason why he shouldn't have kept a key of the house, dropped Wakefield that evening, gone to his flat and established his presence there, crept out by some back way, murdered Benson, returned in the small hours, and received Duncan's telephone call as if nothing had happened. On the other hand I liked Peter and found in him that rare quality in any modern—sincerity. Beef liked him too, and Beef's instincts were apt to lead him well.

3. *Wakefield*. In character, the nearest thing I could recognize as a potential murderer, at any rate among those I had met in the case, but again with no known motive.

4. *Duncan*. Duncan had hanged himself, but I was induced to take the police view that he had done this rather than reveal all he knew, and not because he was ashamed of some act of his. I couldn't see Duncan jabbing at Benson with that knife in any case. And if he had committed the murder, how was it that Stewart had, apparently, shown Benson out of the front door himself?

5. *Mrs. Duncan*. Well, if ever a woman were capable physically of committing a murder, this one looked as though she were. But what conceivable motive could she

have? And why should she be suspected rather than anyone who had passed the Cypresses at any time on foot? It was true she was one of those in the house, and the only one of them (except Stewart of course) who looked powerful enough to have done it. But that was all that one could say.

6. *Rose and Freda*. It would really have been very far-fetched to think of these two as possible murderesses merely because they were employed in the house where a murder had been committed.

7. *Ed Wilson*. If anyone in this tangle might be considered a suspect, he had to be. But again, one could see no possible motive. He had been more sympathetic in his attitude towards Benson than any of the others, who cordially disliked the man. And although he had no alibi, he stood to gain nothing so far as one could see.

8. *The mechanic*. He had admittedly been up to the house at twelve o'clock that night, but beyond that had no connecting point. I liked his easy manner and open face, and personally refused to suspect him.

9. *Wilkinson*. Now there was a man one felt physically, morally and mentally capable of murdering another man with very little concrete motive. He had the sourness and strength of the old type of villain, and from the first moment that Beef had gone into his pub and seen how badly kept and uninviting it was, how the beer pipes from the cellar needed cleaning, and the beer itself was none of the best, from that moment Beef had decided that he was an "unsatisfactory character" and had had, he assured me, "an eye on him from the start." He admittedly went up to the house at frequent intervals, and would not tell us when he had last been there, but again there was no known motive. If Beef's pretty interpretation of Omar Khayyám's reference to the

surly Tapster had anything in it, this man's connection
with the murder might yet be established.

10. *Sheila Benson.* She had given us our most puzzling
interview. Her blatant disregard for decency was so
conspicuous as almost to be thought a bluff. Her evidence had been perfectly clear, but it conflicted with so
much else that we had heard. Was she really in love with
Peter, as she said? Could she really have scarcely
known Stewart, as she claimed? And when she told us
that the doctor was indifferent to her infidelities, was
she speaking the truth? Those seemed important questions to probe.

11. *The old man.* I remembered Ed Wilson's admission
of having met, on the morning after the murder, an old
man leaving the main gate. Had he any connection with
the "second figure" seen by Rose from the landing window? Or was he some harmless tramp who had slept in
the summerhouse that night? If the former, it seemed
possible that he was the murderer. If the latter, he might
have very valuable information.

12. *Orpen, or Oppenstein.* He had no connection with
the murder, of course, but was a name I remembered,
since it had interested Beef, and been remembered by
the cook.

Chapter XIII

W HEN Beef was what he somewhat ambiguously called "on the job," his old habits were apt to return to him, and he liked to work regular hours. In this at least, I felt, he was original, for every other detective, of whose exploits I had read, would examine foot-prints, if possible, by moonlight, and make quite ordinary inquiries in the small hours with all the business of Grand Guignol. Beef would arrive at his headquarters—usually the scene of the murder—with great punctuality at ten o'clock, take an hour off for what he pompously termed his dinner, and leave the place promptly at six. This did not mean, of course, that he would not, on occasion, do a little nocturnal prowling, or early-morning observation. But he had to have good reason for it beyond the providence of inexpensive colour for his biographer.

That next day he was in a silent, self-important mood when I met him, and told me solemnly that he had "one or two investigations to carry out." When I tried to discover the nature of these, he told me that I "would see," and said no more until we arrived at Sydenham.

At the Cypresses he asked at once for Ed Wilson,

and the young man came to us in the library. I
noticed a remarkable change in his manner from
the last time I had seen him. Instead of the rather
aggressive, almost cheeky young man whom we
had interviewed, this was a jumpy and apprehensive Wilson, who seemed afraid of each question
before it was put to him.

"You've got nothing else to tell me?" asked Beef,
eyeing him narrowly.

"No, Sergeant," he said, and shook his head
with uncharacteristic vigour.

"Sure?" persisted Beef.

"Why, what do you think I might have?" returned
Wilson, a little of the old aggression in his manner
again.

"All right," said Beef, "we'll leave it at that.
Only, if you *have* got anything up your sleeve, I'd
advise you friendly to out with it. Now then, I want
to see that summer-house."

Ed Wilson seemed genuinely surprised. "Summer-
house?" he repeated.

"Yes. That summer-house where you told me it
would be possible for an old tramp to spend the
night."

"Oh yes," said Wilson, "I remember."

Beef picked up his hat, and we followed the
chauffeur to the front door. "Nasty sort of a morning," commented Beef, as a gust of damp wind
caught our faces in that gloomy drive. Neither of
us replied as we took the gravel path beside the
windows which led to a small lawn which might

once have been used for croquet, at the back of the house. We crossed this and found, half-concealed by the shrubs beyond it, one of those damp-looking, rotting little structures which the gardeners of fifty years ago loved to put in the most conspicuous points of their gardens. It seemed more a shed than a summer-house, and even before he opened the door, I knew the smell of rotting wood, and foresaw the stacks of miscellaneous garden tools and ornaments which we should find inside. I was right too—the place did not seem to have been used for anything but storing for many years, and I could smell the damp in the floor-boards.

Beef sniffed the air with the vigour of a vacuum-cleaner being demonstrated by a young and ardent salesman. "Hm," he said, and then looked round him. After a moment he stooped down and picked up three or four small pieces of paper. These were about an inch by three-quarters of an inch, with one long edge straight and the opposite edge charred, the two ends being roughly torn. He took them between his thick finger and thumb and then placed them carefully in the pages of his notebook. "Good," he grunted, wishing no doubt to be enigmatic.

Replacing his notebook in his pocket, he ignored the rest of the shed and, standing in the doorway, he began to examine the ground over which we had come.

"Now, if anyone was to want to get from here to the front gate at night," he said, "when it didn't matter whether they were seen from the windows of the house or not, that's the way they'd take, isn't it?" and he pointed obliquely across the lawn. "If, on the other hand," he continued sagaciously, "they was to be creeping out in the morning, under full observation from the windows, they'd probably go round that way, wouldn't they?" and he indicated what might have been a path running round under the trees at the side of the lawn, so reaching the gate. "We'll follow them both," he said finally.

"But Beef," I interrupted, thinking this clumsy reasoning was a part of his façade, "what on earth do you expect to find now? If those foot-prints you asked about ever had been there, they would have been washed away long ago."

"I'm not looking for foot-prints," returned Beef. He started to pace across the lawn in the way he had first suggested, with his large, rheumy eyes watching the ground near him. He got as far as the front gate without pausing, and returned to the summer-house. "Now the other one," he said, and he repeated the same performance with the second of the two routes, still, apparently, finding nothing. "That's funny," he commented, inevitably, and stood pulling gently at the damp ends of his moustache.

Presently he began to cogitate slowly again. "Now if anyone following that route was to come on anything that had been thrown away by anyone else who had been leaving by the ordinary way, where would they have been most likely to find it?"

"In the attic," I suggested helpfully.

"No, don't let's have any larking about," said Beef; "this is serious. Can't you see what I'm getting at? There must be somewhere, where something thrown from there might be come on by somebody going this way."

"Well," I admitted, "I suppose that might be so, but it still leaves a fairly large area to cover. If they walked down the drive from the front door to the gate they could easily reach at least ten yards of this shrubbery which would be passed through by a person leaving the summer-house."

"All right, then, those ten yards we'll have to search," said Beef, and the two of us obediently followed him into the bushes.

"What are we to look for?" I asked.

"Anything," said Beef.

"Well, there are plenty of dead leaves," I returned sarcastically.

"Anything out of the way," Beef amplified.

Suddenly there was a triumphant cry from Wilson, who had been a little way from us. "Would you call this out of the way?" he cried, and opening his hand under Beef's nose he showed him a small, unrusted latch-key.

Beef grabbed it. "Yes, I should," he said; "only it wasn't what I was expecting to find." He stared narrowly at Wilson. "Not by a long chalk," he added.

We searched for a little longer in a desultory sort of way, and then Beef announced that we had done enough. But when we had returned to the library he sat drumming his fingers on the desk in a vacant and irritating way until I asked him what he was going to do next.

"I think," he announced, "I'll go down to see that bank manager. I've often said it was time I took my money out of the savings bank and had it in some place where I could write cheques. Now I've set up on my own it would be better, I daresay. And while I'm on it I might as well ask this manager what to do."

We therefore drove to the local branch of one of the Big Five, and Beef produced his card and asked to see the manager. "You wait here," he said rather rudely to me when he was summoned to the end of the counter.

I didn't have to wait long, for the brisk and busy manager seemed to dispose of him with great promptitude.

"Did you get the information you wanted?" I asked.

"He wasn't very chatty," regretted Beef, "but he gave me all I needed. These are the dates on which Stewart drew those sums in notes," and he showed me a written list. "Now, what I want to know is where Benson happened to be when each of those was drawn."

"You'd better go and ask Mrs. Benson," I suggested slyly.

"No, thanks," almost shouted Beef. "I had a dose of her yesterday. I'm going to do it on the telephone." And I waited outside the booth while he shouted into the instrument.

When at last he joined me, he said, "It's a funny thing, but the third of those was drawn while that doctor was on his month's holiday. He had a lock-out here while he was away."

"A lock-out?" I repeated.

"That's what she said."

After a moment I understood. "Oh, you mean a *locum*. A *locum tenens*."

"You know I can't speak French," growled Beef, "and anyway it's time we had a tumble down the sink."

I sighed. "All right," I conceded, "if you're satisfied with your morning's work."

"I am," said Beef, suddenly cheering up, "more than satisfied. This case isn't going to be as difficult as what I thought for." And he turned abruptly into a large and lavishly decorated public-house.

But I was relieved to find that in his mood of busy preoccupation, Beef did not waste as much time as usual in leaning conversationally over the bar, and we found ourselves strolling back towards the Cypresses before it was yet closing-time. I was reflecting that these were the dog-days of the case, the period after we had heard its more or less exciting outline, and before there were sensational developments. I realized that one had to plod through these steady hours of investigation, but Beef's nature made the process a somewhat too realistic one.

However, he suddenly stopped, and became so demonstrative as to seize my arm. "Cor, look at that!" he said, and there was a thrill of real excitement in his voice.

We were standing outside the window of a small second-hand shop, one of those useful and satisfactory little businesses so pleasantly different from their refined rich cousins the antique shops. I thought that at least he had seen in its window some object through which he could confidently expect to trace the murderer. Benson's own watch perhaps, or something of the sort. But to my disgust I found that his finger was stretched out in eager indication of a second-hand dart-board.

"Just what I've been looking for," he said. "Nice elm board, hardly been played on, marked seven-and-six. Almost too good to be true; they're worth twenty-five bob new, and last a lifetime if you take care of them. Mind you, you want to soak them in water every week, otherwise they dry and little bits fall off of them. Then you should shift the numbers round now and again so as you don't get the nineteen and twenty worn to shreds. But handled carefully, a board like that'll be played on when I'm pushing up the daisies. It's just what I want for that front room of mine. I told Mrs. Beef when she was arranging all those antimacassars and things that I should add *my* little note of decoration to the room before long, and this is just what I had in mind. I don't say she'll be pleased, mind you, to have a dart-board up beside the photo of her father.

I remember her saying once before when I wanted it that she was afraid the glass would get broke. But there you are, she'll have to lump it. Come on, let's go in and buy it. It'll go in the back of your car quite handy."

I got over my disappointment at finding that this had been all there was to excite Beef, and followed him into the shop. It was a dingy little place, full of valueless glass and china, a few Victorian chairs, some spring mattresses standing against the wall, a couple of chests of drawers that scarcely left one room to move around the shop, and all the useless bric-à-brac that one finds in such places. It smelt stale and unpleasant as though most of the furniture, before it had been scattered by auction sales, had stood around the shuttered bedrooms of Sydenham, while their late possessors had lain awaiting the undertaker on their brass bedsteads.

A sort of cracked cow-bell on a rusty spring sounded flatly as Beef pushed the door open, and after a minute's delay a little, sallow man, still gently masticating portions of the lunch which he had left in the back room, was blinking at us from behind steel-rimmed spectacles. The scanty grey hair on his head was like thin lichen, and his moustache had a hopeless droop. "Yes," he said, concentrating in that syllable all the resignation in the world, all the indifference to the rest of humanity, to past and future, to beauty and sorrow, that could have been voiced in a long, diffuse poem by a disgruntled modern poet. He had no hope of us, or of anything else. He was prepared, without enthusiasm, to take our money; without either courtesy or discourtesy, hurry or distaste, to hear what we wanted; and he was absolutely determined that he would go to no trouble in the matter of serving us, or feel the slightest disappointment if we spent nothing at all.

In contrast, Beef's gusto was almost adolescent. "That dart-board," he gasped, grinning.

"Seven-and-six," said the man passionlessly.

"I'll have it," said Beef. "Would you wrap it up for me?"

"I don't know whether I've got any paper," said the shopkeeper as he wearily brought the dart-board from the window.

"Newspaper would do," said Beef enthusiastically.

"I'll see," said the shopkeeper, and disappeared through his private door again.

Beef gave his head a characterisitc sideways jerk and said, "There you are." Then, as he got no response from me, he began once again to look round the shop. His eye fell on an earthenware pot like a long piece of glazed and coloured drain-pipe, such as one still finds used for umbrellas in the front halls of vicarages. It was not, however, this piece of earthenware which had attracted Beef, but the collection of sticks, whips and umbrellas which it held. Presently, with a gurgle of pleasure, he drew out one of these objects and held it up to me. "Do you know what that is?" he said.

I confessed that I did not.

"It's a swordstick," said Beef in a low and conspiratorial voice. "Wouldn't half be useful for anyone engaged in my work, would it? I mean I really ought to have something like that. You never know what characters I may come up against, and anything like that would come in handy at an awkward moment. I applied for a licence to carry firearms the other day, but they said I hadn't sufficient grounds. Still, I think I ought to have something of this sort. How much do you think it would cost?"

I sighed. "I've no idea," I said. "But really, I think that at your age you should be too old for toys."

"No, but I mean, you never know, do you?" said Beef, "I'll just ask the price."

Just then the shopkeeper returned. "How much is this?" Beef said, showing him the article.

"Ten shillings," he was told.

A little damped, but not finally discouraged, he continued to pull the blade in and out. "Lot of money," he commented; "do you think you could take less?"

"No, I couldn't," said the shopkeeper. "It cost me seven-and-six."

"Still, you'll have a job to get half a quid for it, won't you?"

"No, I shan't," said the shopkeeper. "I've only had it ten days. It'll go all right."

"I wonder where you'd buy a thing like that?" asked Beef inquisitively. "I mean it's not what you'd expect to find in Sydenham, is it?"

"I don't know," said the shopkeeper, again appearing fatigued. "I bought that from an old chap who brought it in here himself. I remember because I was having breakfast at the time."

"Oh," said Beef thoughtfully, "it was early in the morning, was it? Ten days ago, was it? That would be about the time when the Sydenham murder took place?"

During this conversation I had been aware of the fact that the lace curtain had more than once been pulled aside from the glass-topped door that led into the private part of the house, and the red face of a middle-aged woman with eager eyes had peered out. At this point its owner, whom I took to be the shopkeeper's wife, could restrain herself no longer and burst into the shop.

"It was the very day it was discovered," said the lady excitedly, "because I remember remarking on it at the time. I asked him if he thought it had anything to do with it."

"I see," said Beef, still thoughtful. "So it was brought in on the morning after the murder, was it? That's interesting. And you say it was brought in by an old tramp? What was he like?"

It was the woman who answered again, her husband seeming to take as little interest in the drama of detection as in all the other vanities and stupidities of human life.

"Oh, he was a regular old tramp," she said, "nasty scruffy old fellow. I didn't like the look of him."

Beef became even more solemn. "That's very interesting," he said.

"Why?" asked the woman eagerly, "are you Something To Do with the case?"

"I'm investigating the matter," said Beef grimly.

"Are you really?" said the woman. "Well, I never." And it was quite obvious that she never had.

She continued to talk. "I'm ever so interested in anything like that," she said, "my husband'll tell you. I've always got my nose in a detective novel. Wouldn't it be funny if this very swordstick turned out to be the evidence you were looking for? I mean it would be nice to think I had something to do with it."

Beef grew grand. "Had you ever seen that tramp before?" he asked loftily.

"Never!" cried the woman. "Had you, Frank?"

"Can't say I had," returned her husband indifferently.

"But I should know him again," she went on.

"You would?" said Beef. "That's good. Now I'll tell you what," he added. "I'm anxious to interview that man in connection with the murder of Doctor Benson. If you was to help me find him you'd be making quite a name for yourself."

"Well! I'll do anything I can to help," said the woman.

"I'll tell you what you can do. If ever you should clap eyes on him again, don't let him out of your sight. Follow him through thick and thin, up hill and down dale, till you find out where he goes."

The picture which Beef's exaggerated phraseology suggested to me was a vivid one. I could see the shopkeeper's wife leaping surreptitiously in the wake of the swordstick-vendor over the greater part of England's main roads until she brought him to earth in some remote workhouse. However, I said nothing as Beef gave his final instructions.

"As soon as you've snared him," he said, "get on the 'phone to me. If I'm not there, tell my wife she must get hold of me as quick as possible. She'll very likely know where I am," he added, less cheerfully, "but don't you forget. There's my number; put it in a safe place. And remember, you may be the means of bringing a criminal to book, saving the life of an innocent man, and getting your photo in the newspapers. Now, I've got important matters to attend to, and I must be getting along."

Suddenly, and quite unexpectedly, the shopkeeper spoke. "What about that stick?" he asked. "Are you going to buy it?"

Beef pulled out a ten-shilling note, and at last we left the shop.

Chapter XIV

"I'T'S time," announced Beef, "that we interviewed a parson."

"A parson?" I repeated, with the air of surprise that is expected of me. "Why a parson?"

"Comic relief," said Beef; "must have a parson. Wouldn't be a case without a parson."

"But you can't just go off like that and interview a parson."

"I don't see why not," said Beef. "I've noticed you enjoy writing about them."

"Still, you mustn't forget," I pointed out, "there's such a thing as realism. This is a murder mystery, not a comedy of manners."

"Well, you never know with parsons," said Beef. "It's a gamble, I grant you. But you might easily learn something handy. They always know everyone else's business, and in a place like this I shouldn't be surprised if he hadn't got some real information. We know that Stewart Ferrers handed money over to him, so there must be some connection."

"All right," I agreed. "I gather it was St. Jocelyn's that the family attended. We'll find out where the vicarage is."

It turned out, however, that the Reverend Percy

Smyke was not at home. "He's with the Scouts," explained the servant knowingly.

"Funny time for scouting," commented Beef.

"Mr. Smyke always takes a week-end camp at this time. He's wonderful with boys, you know."

"Where would it be?" asked Beef, and being told that it was at Sevenoaks, he asked me to drive him down there in the car. We found the St. Jocelyn's Troop encamped on a piece of level pasture-land, well secluded from the nearest road. Three small tents seemed all that were visible, but there was evidently a great deal of organization and sign-writing necessary for their maintenance. On a board was scribbled the word "Latrines," with an arrow pointing towards the wood. On another was "Officer's Tent," while the two remaining tents were labelled "Crocodiles" and "Titmice."

A number of perspiring boys wore, not only uniform, but an assortment of impedimenta—utensils, a complete armoury of knives and hatchets, rolls of blankets, cameras, kettles and sport clothes. Some of them had evidently just arrived. As we walked over to the group they seemed mildly curious about their two strange visitors. And when Beef asked if Mr. Smyke could be found they answered in chorus that he was in his tent. Their excitement grew terrific as one shouted "Smykie," and the others dashed towards the tent labelled "Officer's."

The vicar finally emerged, followed by a small boy with curly chestnut hair and an ingratiating smile. Mr. Smyke resembled Señor Largo Caballero, having large sunburnt ears and protuberant blue eyes. His clothes were designed to exhibit a pair of ageing, though sunburnt, knees and a tuft of manly grey hair on the torso.

"Mr. Smyke?" inquired Beef unnecessarily.

"Indeed, yes," said the parson. "You're one of the boys' fathers, I suppose. Well, here we all are. You can choose your son," he added heartily.

"No. If I *had* a son," Beef explained, "he wouldn't be dancing around here dressed up like a Boer soldier. But it's not that that I wanted to see you about. I'm Sergeant Beef, late of His Majesty's Police Force."

"Oh, I see," said Mr. Smyke. "And what can I do for you?"

"I'm investigating the murder of Doctor Benson."

The vicar seemed to find this happy news, and smiled broadly. "Ah, the murder," he said. "Quite. Charmed, I'm sure. Anything I can do. Delighted. Quite a pleasure."

"I don't know whether there is," said Beef, "but I thought there might be. Did you know any of the family well?"

"Mr. Stewart Ferrers," explained the vicar, "was a very good Christian. He supported our projects most helpfully. He bought us, in fact, one of those tents when we were a little overcrowded last year, and he has always been most willing to come to my assistance in any little matter I have in hand."

"Did you know his brother?" asked Beef.

"I did," said Mr. Smyke, and his voice had that

plummy quality which sometimes comes with public speaking. "Quite a different type, however. A worldlier character altogether. Most unfortunate political tenets, I believe. I have found that the modern tendency to condone poorly disguised communism undermines much of my work here. The boys get Ideas from some of the masters in the local schools which I greatly deplore, and lately our troop has shrunk in numbers."

Beef interrupted. "But you're not blaming Mr. Peter Ferrers for that, surely?" he said.

"Oh no," said Mr. Smyke, "he's not in my parish. But it's the general tendency, the general tendency. And one fostered by that atheistic periodical of his."

"And Doctor Benson?" asked Beef. "What was your opinion of him?"

Mr. Smyke hesitated. "I really scarcely know what to say. *De mortuis*, you know. *De mortuis*. But I can't say that I was by any means an admirer of his methods."

"His methods?" persisted Beef. "What was wrong with his methods?"

At this point we were interrupted by a small boy with a piece of stick in his hand who asked if Mr. Smyke was ready for him to pass his fire-lighting test. Whereat an enormous smile passed over the vicar's features as he gently patted the boy's shoulder. "In a few moments, Archie," he said kindly, and turning apologetically to us, "such little enthusiasts," he murmured. "Full of life. Full of fun. The pleasantest part of my work."

"You were saying," grunted Beef.

"Oh yes, about Doctor Benson. Excellent, no doubt, scientifically most efficient, but not, I regret to say, orthodox."

The word defeated Beef. "How do you mean?" he asked.

"Unchristian doctrines," explained the vicar with a quick shake of his head as though he were enjoying the suspense.

"Such as?"

"Chiefly on the subject of burial."

"Burial?"

"Yes, indeed, burial."

"I didn't know there were any doctrines on the subject of burial. I mean, I thought when you'd snuffed it, you'd snuffed it. And when you were dead you were finished with all that sort of thing."

The parson gave him a patronizing smile. "You may find that you're just, in a sense, beginning with it. But in any case I was speaking of the corporal remains. Dust to dust, ashes to ashes, you know," and he sadly shook his head, while with his right forefinger he scratched the back of his sunburnt knee. "Perhaps you'll just excuse me while I give the boys something to do. Crocodiles! Now, boys, peg your brailing down, there's a storm coming up. And you, Titmice," he said to an oafish young man with an incipient moustache and his bespectacled junior, "light the fire. We've got to have some cocoa."

A gentle activity began, though the members of the St. Jocelyn's Troop were evidently impatient for the return of their scoutmaster.

The vicar returned to us. "Now then," he said brightly.

"I want to clear up this matter of burial," said Beef. "What was it you didn't like about his views?"

"Ah, yes," said the vicar, "cremation, I'm afraid." He breathed the word as though he were confiding some unmentionable crime. "He was a staunch advocate of that offensive modern heresy."

"What's wrong with it?" asked Beef. "Healthy, I should call it."

The vicar shuddered. "We don't need to go into that, " he said. "It disposes of the prescribed ceremonies of burial." He turned abruptly to the two members of the Titmouse Patrol. "Now, Moo," he said, "not more than two matches, remember," and added in explanation to us, "we always call him Moo."

I was tempted to ask for a reason, but Beef's unimaginative face discouraged me.

"So Benson believed in cremation?" said Beef, who was working under difficulties.

"I'm afraid so," said the vicar, "ardently, in fact."

"Has he always done so?"

"For some time now," returned Mr. Smyke. "The Ferrers' old nurse who died three or four years ago was first cremated, though I understood that she herself had, in a weak moment, expressed some half-delirious wish for it, fearing, apparently, that she would be buried alive. Then their father and a garden boy who worked for them up till a year ago were also cremated. And lately there has been nothing short of an epidemic of it in my parish. All by Benson's recommendation. I've suffered—in spirit of course," he added brightly and finally.

"Benson wasn't a churchgoer?" said Beef.

"I'm sorry to say he was not. You know that lately congregations everywhere have fallen off. Cinemas opening and such. It's a bad example to the boys, a very bad example, when elder people no longer trouble to attend our services. We need half a dozen recruits to the choir as it is, and the boys' club is practically empty in the evenings. A great pity."

I could see that Beef was fighting to keep his temper while he listened to these perpetual discursions. "Did he ever explain it to you?" he asked the vicar.

"How could he? It was heresy of course, rank heresy. Why, the garden boy whom I mentioned was in my choir, a most promising treble. I knew the parents well, but Benson had put his word in and they had made their decision. What could I do? The poor little fellow was incinerated."

"There's something else I'd like to ask you," said Beef after a pause. . . .

As we stood talking the members of the two patrols, some seven in number in all, had gradually been creeping nearer to Mr. Smyke, like the woodland animals in *Snow White and the Seven*

Dwarfs. Anxious not to appear impertinently inquisitive about our conversation, they had yet felt the need of their master's presence and now began to hang round him like bats on a barn beam. One had seized his hand and stood toying with it as though it were a puppy that had been given to him, while others formed a rough semicircle in the centre of which the vicar stood facing us, his arm on the shoulder of his next door neighbour.

"And what is that?" he asked blandly.

"It's about these stories that have been going round," said Beef. "Have you heard anything?"

"Stories?" queried the vicar.

Beef adopted his own manner. "Yes, morality and that," he whispered.

"I don't know what you mean," exclaimed Mr. Smyke.

"I mean Stewart Ferrers and Mrs. Benson. At least, that's what I heard."

"Ah, that," said the vicar. "Yes, whispers had reached me, but I make a point of totally ignoring such things. I have it on the best authority that the two of them were seen alone in a car parked off the road on that new building estate near my house. I was also told that they had attended dances together quite flagrantly, and that a separation between Benson and his wife had been under discussion. But, of course, I never listen to rumours. Never," he repeated emphatically.

"But you had heard them. And what about Peter and Mrs. Benson? Had that reached your ears?"

"What, another suggestion? No, I'm bound to say I hadn't heard *that*," said the vicar with interest. "Is there anything in it, do you think?"

"I don't know," said Beef, "I was hoping you'd be able to tell me."

"No, it's quite new to me, quite new," said Mr. Smyke, inferring that it was none the worse for that, but probably even more stirring.

Beef threw his eyes for the first time over the encampment. "Well, you seem to be nicely settled here," he said.

"Ah, yes," said the vicar, "splendid fellows. Full of gusto. Full of *joie de vivre*. Pleasantest aspect of my job. Jolly lads. Happy days."

The last phrase aroused a faint revival in Beef's fading interest, for he imagined it to be a toast. But realizing his mistake, he shook hands hastily with the vicar, and we returned to the car.

Chapter XV

BUT when we got back to the Cypresses, we found serious news awaiting us. I, personally, was not displeased that Beef should be pulled up by something more relevant and more earnest, for this gadding about, talking to all sorts of unnecessary people, seemed to me a waste of time, and one which would, eventually, exasperate the man who was employing him.

It was Peter himself who told us. "A very strange thing has happened," he said when we met him in the gloomy hall of his house.

"I know," said Beef; "that publican what used to be your gardener has confessed to the whole thing."

Peter did not smile. "Ed Wilson, our chauffeur, has completely disappeared," he said.

Beef dropped into a chair. "Oh, he has, has he? The silly young fool. I thought that might happen."

"But you surely don't suspect him of murdering Benson, do you?" said Peter Ferrers with some concern.

"Suspect is a word I never use. Either I know a thing, or I don't, and that's all there is to it. I don't believe in suspicions, they lead you into all sorts of funny places."

"But did he commit the murder?" asked Peter Ferrers.

"I don't know," said Beef. "I don't know yet who did commit that murder. But I don't want to lose Wilson's evidence. What do the police say about it?"

"Oh, the police don't seem to worry very much," said Peter Ferrers. "Stute told me this morning he was very sorry, but he had all the evidence he needed with or without young Wilson."

Beef made a scornful sound. "But how does he account for his having gone off, then?" he said. "A man doesn't sneak away for nothing."

"Well, they don't seem to think there's any need to account for it. It appears that Wilson had a liaison with the girl here, and it may easily be that, like so many unattached young men, he found it easier to disappear than to let that attachment take him any nearer to matrimony."

"I see, that's what Stute thinks, is it?" said Beef. "Well, where is this girl? I'd like to have a word with her."

Peter rang the bell, but it was Freda who answered. "Yes," she said, puffing noisily, for she had evidently run all the way upstairs.

"Send Rose in, will you?"

"Rose, sir? She said you knew she was off. She left half an hour ago, with her suitcase and all."

Beef chuckled. "There goes Stute's theory again. She's gone to join Wilson, that's what she's done. The two of them have been hand in glove for a long time."

Peter Ferrers seemed completely at a loss. "Whoever else I suspected of the crime," he said, "I never thought Wilson had anything to do with it. He was a thoroughly decent young fellow, and the girl, so far as I knew her, was straight and pleasant. I can't understand it at all."

"I don't know why you should suppose now," said Beef, "that they're mixed up in the murder, just because they've chosen this time to run away together."

"It's precisely that," said Peter Ferrers. "The fact that they have chosen this time. Wilson must know that he calls suspicion down on himself."

"Then the best thing I can do," said Beef, "is to find them."

Peter Ferrers smiled. "I certainly agree with you," he said. "That at least would be useful work."

"It may mean expense," warned Beef.

"That's all right. I have my brother's authority to meet expenses within reason."

"Very well then, I'll do my best. Though I shouldn't count too much on it helping your brother, Mr. Ferrers. Even if I do catch this young Wilson, as catch him I will, I haven't any great faith in what he can tell us."

Beef slammed his notebook, stood up, and marched towards the front door with me hurrying after him.

"Where now?" I asked, as he crawled into the car.

"Edgware,' he said. "I've got the sister's address. We'll see what she says about this. The silly young fellow. Still, there may be no great harm done."

I was not present at Beef's interview with Wilson's sister, but I gathered when he returned to the car that it had been a successful one. She had always found it difficult, it appeared, to make Ed Wilson out. He was too ambitious by half, and meant to get somewhere, whatever stood in his way. But she didn't believe he'd have done anything terrible, and she was sure he had nothing to do with the murder.

He had certainly seemed a little on edge since it had happened, but that, the sister had assured Beef, was only natural. He had not told her that he was going away, and certainly at no time had talked of the place to which he might go. I asked Beef if he believed that, and he said that he did. He knew when anyone was lying to him, and Wilson's sister had been speaking the truth. One thing that he had elicited from her was that Wilson, at any rate to the best of her knowledge—and she said she could be pretty certain on that point—had never had a passport. If he had he'd taken it out in the last few days.

Beef thoughtfully returned home, and I went with him. In these last few days he had grown so reserved, at any rate about the conclusions he was drawing, that I no longer tried to press him. But I did not feel it was a very hopeful Beef who stepped across to his telephone and got himself in connection with Scotland Yard.

"I want to speak to Inspector Stute," I heard him shout into the instrument. "Stute," he repeated, "S-T-U-T-E," and after a long pause, "Inspector Stute," I heard him say again. Without troubling to put his hand over the mouthpiece he said aside to me, "Bad organization. Now if they'd offered me a post there, as they might well have done when I'd found two murderers for them, I'd soon have seen things were efficient.... Is that Inspector Stute?" he suddenly bellowed.

The conversation that followed had best be spared the reader. It consisted of a clumsy and repetitive persuasion by Beef to get Stute to do what he wanted. It appeared that only with his authority could the passport office be approached in order to ascertain whether Wilson had obtained a document within the last few weeks. Beef used every argument in his power, since Stute was, presumably, most unwilling. He started with man-to-man professionalism as though he never doubted the other's acquiescence. He then tried heavy-footed flattery, saying that a man of Stute's eminence would scarcely mind doing a little thing like that for a beginner. He went on to argue that it was only fair, and used the extraordinary word "sporting" to suggest that if Stute did not comply he would be taking an advantage over a confrère who had not the facilities of the Yard. Finally, and perhaps most effectively, he made a modest plea on the grounds that Peter Ferrers had particularly asked him to find Wilson, and that, apart from any question of the case, he wanted to carry out the wishes of the man who was employing him. It seemed that this won the unwilling inspector, and he put down the receiver with a sigh of relief. "He'll ring through and tell me in a few minutes. Soon as ever he's been on to the passport office," he said. "We'll soon know."

"Have you any idea at all?" I asked him.

"Only something his sister let slip. She doesn't know where he is, but she does know he's abroad."

I smiled. "That covers a fairly large area," I said.

"Not if he hadn't got a passport, it doesn't," returned Beef triumphantly. "There's only two or three trips he could have gone on that I know of, and at the most it's three or four."

We sat there waiting silently and grimly for the telephone to ring. Mrs. Beef, a woman of great compassion as far as I was concerned, brought us in two large cups of tea, which I should have enjoyed more if it had not been for Beef's somewhat noisy habits of drinking any hot beverage, which contrasted with his easy and silent disposal of beer.

When at last the bell rang, his replies were limited to knowing negatives: "He didn't?" "No, I thought he wouldn't." And finally there was a somewhat fulsome expression of gratitude.

Beef turned to his reference shelf. "Keep all these handy," he said with a wink at me. "Time-tables from all over Europe," and I saw the English and the Continental Bradshaws.

"Now presuming that that girl was going to join him," he said artfully, "she'd be hopping off tonight, wouldn't she?"

"That's if she's not returning to her home, going to another job, staying in London, or one of the hundred and one things she may have left the Cypresses to do," I said coldly.

"She's after him," pronounced Beef. "Otherwise why did she sneak off sudden like that? Now you listen to what I'm saying. What we've got to do is to watch all the boat trains from Victoria what leave today. She's almost sure to go from there. In case she doesn't we can get Stute to put some men on the direct lines, or on the ports would be better in case she tried to go down by bus or something. But it's pretty sure to be Victoria. You and I will be watching all the trains, and watching them well."

I could picture it. Beef watching a train was Beef "on the job." I half expected him to suggest disguises, or at least coloured glasses to wear when he took up his position on the platform. But I said nothing.

"If we see her," he said, "it's the Continent for us. And even if we don't, I don't see we should be doing any harm having a run over for a look round."

"But, Beef," I said, "is that altogether fair? Peter Ferrers certainly agreed to pay expenses, but this virtually amounts to a holiday. And you know perfectly well. . ."

"I know perfectly well what I'm doing," said Beef. "Didn't Stute find out what he wanted in that last case by us slipping over to Paris?"

"That was entirely different, and you know it."

"I know I'm going to lay hands on this young fellow, and I know how I'm going to do it. If you don't want to come, say so. If you want to miss the best bit of action you're likely to get over this case— me pursuing a runaway chauffeur in a Continental resort—then stay at home by all means. But if you take my advice, you'll come with me to Victoria."

I took his advice.

Chapter XVI

W<small>E</small> took up our positions near the entrance of the Continental boat-train departure platform, but I was surprised and rather disappointed to find that Beef at first behaved with a sobriety and conventionality that was most uncharacteristic of him. He had bought an evening paper, and held it spread in front of him. And although his eyes were over the top of it as soon as a new group of passengers approached the platform, he made no ostrich-like attempt to conceal himself behind it.

I felt the whole thing was rather forlorn. There was, as Beef had pointed out, a reasonably fair chance that the girl would join Wilson. But since Beef appeared to have elicited from Wilson's sister that the chauffeur was abroad, it was also quite possible that she would be crossing the Channel. One could further assume that since she had left her job today she would be making the journey tonight. And one could guess that she would be leaving Victoria. But each of these was no more than a probability, and for each of them I could have suggested half a dozen alternatives. However, the eternal optimism of Beef was infectious, and I found myself watching the faces of everyone who approached, half expecting to find Rose among them.

We had not been waiting for more than twenty minutes before Beef turned to me with a familiar look on his face.

"Well," he said, "there are only two trains she could be going on tonight. The first one's the eight-twenty for the Newhaven-Dieppe crossing, and the other one isn't till eleven. That's the Dover-Ostend."

"But what about the trains that went before we got here?" I objected, for we had not arrived at the station until well after seven.

"There weren't none," said Beef triumphantly. "At least, none that she could have gone on. The Folkestone-Boulogne was at four-thirty and she couldn't have got that—not without leaving the Cypresses before she did. No, it's one of these two, or none at all tonight." He looked up at the station clock, and then came to the point which I had foreseen nearly five minutes before.

"Quarter to eight," he said thoughtfully. "Well, that about gives me time...Here," he suddenly said with decision, "you hang on here for a bit. I've just got to slip across the platform."

This, at least, I had anticipated, and it was with no surprise at all that I saw him disappear into the buffet. I decided that even where I stood I might be noticeable to anyone approaching the ticket-collector, and took my place on a crowded seat from which I could equally well observe, but where, unless I was being actually sought for, I should remain unnoticed.

Ten minutes later Beef emerged, and crossing to me, took a place beside me that scarcely had room for him, and to obtain possession of which he had to do a good deal of pushing and expanding. He pulled up his newspaper again and nudged me too violently with his elbow.

"Won't half be all right if we have to go across, will it?" he said. "I've only been once, and that was to Paris when I was in the Force and under Stute's orders. He didn't seem to know how to enjoy himself either. If you and me was on our own I believe we'd see life."

I felt that a rather prim attitude befitted me here. "I hope we shall see Wilson," I said curtly; "that, after all, is what we're being paid to go for. There's a girl coming across now who looks rather like Rose. Keep your eyes open."

Beef kept his eyes open in a most conspicuous way, by slumping down into his chair, pulling his hat forward, and peering over the top of his paper like a child playing peep-bo. A little slim man on his left who had been watching him, and feeling the discomfort of his presence for some time, turned and asked him whatever was the matter.

"Investigation," he whispered, "on a big case." Whereat the little man looked extremely uncomfortable, got up, and walked away.

The girl came nearer, and it was evident that she was making for our platform.

"Doesn't look like her to me," said Beef, and he was quite right. "Ah, well, you never know," he added, and we sat on there in silence, until there was only five minutes left to the time at which the train was scheduled to leave.

"I told you it would be no good," I said irritably as the barriers closed and we watched the guard waving.

But Beef was too sanguine to be dismayed yet. "There's the Dover-Ostend train yet," he told me. "I don't say I'd rather go to Belgium than France, but it would be better than nothing. Come on, we've got time to go and have one," and he marched me off the station.

I was thoroughly fatigued when once more we stood waiting for the eleven-o'clock train. And I think that perhaps I dozed off, for I was awakened by a violent nudging from Beef. "Here she comes," he muttered. "Don't let her see you. Do your boot-lace up."

"It's done up," I returned innocently.

"Hide your face, for God's sake," Beef went on rudely, "we don't want her to see us."

His paper was crinkling with his excitement, and his eyes popping over the top of it. "Yes, it's her," he said. "She's quite alone and got her suitcase." His remarks took the form of an American wireless commentary. "She's coming across. She's looking round about. Now she's stopped. She's looking for her ticket. She's got it all right. What did I tell you? She's going to the train. She's showing the man her ticket. He's passed it. She's walking up the platform. I'll keep an eye on her while you hop back and buy two first-class tickets for Ostend."

"First class?" I queried dampingly at the end of this monologue. "Why first-class?"

"Well, I'm a first-class detective, aren't I? I'm not going to do anything by halves."

"I'm not suggesting half-measures," I returned, "but you're spending someone else's money."

"Do you think Lord Simon Plimsoll would go third class?" was his scornful reply. "You get the tickets quick while I watch her."

My last glimpse as I turned to the booking-office was of Beef stalking up the platform with his body slightly crooked and his hat almost meeting his coat-collar.

But I really was impressed. I had to admit that however much one laughed at the old boy it was he and not Stute who had foreseen this, and who was on the track of whatever developments there might be at the end of this journey. His methods seemed ingenuous, but once again I had to admit that they were getting him there.

I walked up the train, peering into the carriages, and almost missed the familiar figure where it crouched in a first-class compartment. As I handed him the ticket, he elaborately destroyed the platform ticket which had admitted him.

"Well, we're off," he said unnecessarily as the train steamed out a few minutes later. "And she's safe and sound in a third-class carriage down the corridor. What do you say to that?"

I said nothing, but I should have respected his achievement more if he had not insisted, every half-hour or so, on walking down the train "to see if she was all right." His manner of passing her carriage was calculated to draw the attention of anyone far less suspicious than Rose might well have been. But apparently it did no harm, and we had the satisfaction of seeing the girl make her way on board at Dover.

Once he had satisfied himself that the gangway was up with Rose still in the third-class quarters, Beef was prepared to relax. "It's only on the films, and in the most improbable detective stories, that they disappear in mid-Channel," he explained as he led me to the bar. "But we must look out for her at Ostend. Can't tell if she's staying there or going on to Brussels. Though since Wilson's sneaked across on an excursion, I should think it's more than likely they're staying on the coast. Garçon," he suddenly shouted to the astonished bar-tender, "two pale ales." Then turning to me. "See, I know a bit of French," he said with a wink.

I was relieved to find that it was a smooth crossing, for I remembered that Beef was not a good sailor. But once the lights of Dover had dimmed, I told him that I was going to turn in.

"All right," he said, "only I think I'd better stay up and keep an eye on things."

I was too tired to ask what things, and took no further interest in the world until I was awakened on our arrival at Ostend to find Beef standing over my bunk. "Come on," he said, "we mustn't lose sight of her."

"Did you enjoy the crossing?" I asked, as I pulled on my shoes.

"Lovely," said Beef poetically, "clear moonlight and no licensing hours."

We once more, as Beef put it, "picked up the trail" in the customs shed, where Rose's modest suitcase was passed more quickly than our own. But outside in the chill half-light of an autumnal dawn I was disappointed to find no sign of Ed Wilson waiting, and commented on it to Beef.

"What did you expect?" he asked scornfully. "Did you think she was going to send telegrams to tell us where he was? Still, I wouldn't mind betting she goes straight to his hotel."

At that moment a taxi came hurrying towards the station and Rose stopped it. She appeared to have some difficulty in explaining to the driver where she wanted to go, and eventually showed him a paper from her bag. Their conversation was out of our earshot, so we could only conclude that she had given him Wilson's address.

Beef looked round for a taxi, but there was none in sight. "Taxi!" he shouted ineffectually, his voice echoing round the almost silent station. What few passengers from our train were staying in the town appeared to have gone already in the several hotel brakes sent down for them, and we were alone in the empty square. There was no sign of any other vehicle, and Beef grew slightly profane.

"Always the same," he said. "Never one when you want it. There she goes over the bridge," and he stood watching the motor-car disappear from sight. "We know she's in the town," he consoled himself, "but it may take us days to find them now." Then brightening a little, "Days!" he added.

Chapter XVII

THE Ostend season was nearly over, but there was still a fair number of English holiday-makers staying in the hotels, and the narrow streets were by no means deserted. Beef chose a modest hotel, I was relieved to find, and we both decided to sleep till lunch-time and to meet then.

We came down to a pleasant meal, but not one, it seemed, which suited Beef. "Little bits of things" was his description, and he used an unprintable metaphor for the beer.

"What are we to do this afternoon?" I asked while we were drinking coffee.

"Well, where would you suppose anyone would get to as had a lot of money to spend in the afternoon?" he replied.

"To the races, I suppose. But why do you ask? Do you suppose Ed Wilson has a lot of money to spend?"

Beef did not condescend to answer my questions. "We'll go to the races," he announced, and there-upon grew silent.

Just then the carillon sounded, and was plainly audible to us where we sat in the pale sunshine in front of our restaurant.

"Nice bells," said Beef, "though I never cared

151

much for church bells at home. What's the idea of
playing tunes on them?"

I began to explain to him something of the tradition of the carillon in the Low Countries, but his
interest had wandered again, for he was taking
advantage of the Continental practice of provid-
ing tooth-picks.

We drove to the race-course in a taxi, and Beef
was astonished at the cheapness of the price of
entry. "Costs you a quid in England," he reflected
as he paid over the modest sum in francs.

We had a most pleasant afternoon, but a totally
fruitless one, enlivened only by two false alarms.
Once we were standing high on the roof of the
grandstand from which the turf and the sea were
equally visible, when Beef thought he recognized
Wilson approaching the Tote. He made a dive for
the stairs, and presently I saw him searching
through the crowd for the man he had picked out,
then, when he saw his mistake, putting his hands
in his pockets and behaving with all the whistling
ingenuousness of a Wallace Beery. The second
time was more embarrassing, for we were together
near the buffet when Beef sprang forward and
clapped his hand on the shoulder of another innocent racegoer. The man turned, revealing an astonished English face, and Beef stuttered his apol-
ogies. "I thought you were someone else," he said
inevitably.

"Well, I'm not," returned the man curtly as he
walked away, and Beef looked very crestfallen.

Finally, his fancy for a horse called Zig-Zag, which came in not only last but several lengths behind its slowest competitor, ended an afternoon which, however unsatisfactory, had at least been healthy and leisurely.

Beef was even more expressively rude about the tea than he had been about the beer, and vowed he would never come abroad again without a couple of pounds of Lipton's in his suitcase. But he cheered up as evening approached and I conceded that the Casino would be the place most likely for anyone with money to spend.

"I wonder," I said sarcastically, "that you have not apparently realized the obvious way to find Wilson."

"What's that?" he asked.

"Go to the Belgian police and get their co-operation. They'd run round the hotel registers in no time."

"Don't be silly. I can't ask them that. I'm here in a private capacity and I've got to find things out for myself. That's all very well for Stute with his letters from South America and such, but we've got to do this job by ourselves. Come on, where's this Casino?"

It seemed to me that if Rose and Ed Wilson were at the Casino at all, it was very probable that only the chauffeur would be at the gaming-tables. We might, I thought, have to find them separately.

"Where else might she be, then?" asked Beef.

"Well, at the concert, for instance."

"What pierrots and that?"

He received my explanation in an impressed silence, and then, when I had finished, "Music," he said, "I like a bit of a tune sometimes."

I took Beef first to the little office at the doors of the gaming-rooms to insure our entry into these when the time came. Fortunately I was a member at Monte Carlo and had my carnet in my pocket-case. This enabled me to get six-day tickets for the two of us. There was an uncomfortable moment when the official asked Beef what club he belonged to.

"Club?" he said, "I've just joined the Marylebone and Paddington Liberal Club, if that's what you mean."

To my relief this was glossed over by the courteous officials and no obstacle was put in our way. But I decided first to visit the concert-hall.

I led Beef to where the orchestra was already playing "a bit of a tune" and we sat down together. Beef folded his arms and sat rapt and silent for about ten minutes. Then he began to refold his arms, shuffle his feet, and out of the corner of my eye I could see his head creeping round trying to see how the people behind were taking it. At last he could contain himself no longer and leaned over towards me. Bringing his mouth close against my ear he said in a hoarse whisper, "When are they going to start?"

"They have started," I said shortly, and handed him the programme, indicating the Ravel Quartet

which they were just then playing. Beef looked at
the printed page in silence for a moment, and then
suddenly slapped his thigh explosively and looked
at me with a huge grin on his face. "Do you know
what I thought?" he said.

But although I did not know what he had thought,
I did not, at that moment, take the offered opportunity of finding out. If Beef had wanted everybody to look at him so that he could see if Rose were
in the hall, he could not have chosen a better
method. But he was oblivious of the white shocked
faces which stared at us in dismay from every side.

"I thought—" he said, still laughing, but I
grasped him firmly by the arms and half guided,
half thrust him out into the foyer.

"You idiot," I said to him violently as soon as we
were outside. "That girl will have warned Wilson
before we can get to the gaming-tables, and then
we shall never be able to catch them."

"Which girl?" asked Beef, bewildered.

"Rose, of course. She was sitting there listening
to the concert until you made a nuisance of yourself," I fumed, "and then of course she turned
round with the rest. Directly she saw you she ran
for the door. If we don't catch them before they get
out of this place we probably never shall."

Beef was still looking dazed as I propelled him
along the corridor, but he had quickly recovered by
the time we reached the wide doors which opened
into the room in which the tables were. Shaking me
loose from his arm like Saul recovering from his fit

as David played to him, he stood with his legs apart and surveyed the room quickly, his eyes travelling over the backs and faces of all the people there.

"Ah," he said suddenly, and moved forward quickly. A moment after him I recognized the back of Wilson's head where he sat, his eyes intent on the table. The pile of counters in front of him seemed evidence that he was playing for high stakes that evening, and Beef stood silently behind him until the wheel had stopped spinning. Then he put his hand on his shoulder as only a policeman can put his hand on a strange man's shoulder. A firm but weary hand, as if weighted by the search, like the tired grip of a falcon as it returns to its master's wrist after an unsuccessful flight.

At this moment there was a disturbance near the door, where Rose had pushed her way past the watchful attendants. But when she saw Beef she stopped and her shoulders seemed to droop slightly. Few of the players had noticed the incident, and the attendants were quite discreet as with quiet, uncaring expressions they pulled back the doors to let the four of us out into the corridor again.

"You silly young fool," said Beef to the chauffeur as soon as we had left the Casino, "whatever possessed you to do a thing like that?"

But Wilson was not to be cowed by this sort of moral lecture from Beef. He was quite as confident now as he had been that day when Beef interviewed him in the library at the Cypresses. "I wanted to see things and get about a bit. Stuck there like a bit of sausage in a toad in the hole. I want to have some fun."

Beef looked at him severely. "You want to read the illustrated Sunday papers," he said, "to see what happens to people like you. Never come to a good end, they don't. And then bringing this girl out," he went on. "Shocking, I call it. What would her people think about it? Living a life of gilded sin. And on the money you took off a dead man too. I don't know how you sleep at nights."

At this phrase Rose gave a short giggle, but she suppressed it immediately.

"And what's more," Beef went on remorselessly, "you're coming back with me by the next boat, that's what you're going to do."

Wilson lit a cigarette and thrust his hands in his pockets. "I've got answers to nearly all of that," he said calmly. "Now in the first place you're not a policeman, so you can't arrest me, and in the second place we're on foreign soil, so you couldn't if you were. I took the money all right. Why not? He didn't need it any more. I didn't think anybody would know he had it on him. Nobody saw me take it anyway, but I suppose if you've got the numbers of the notes you can prove that against me all right."

"I can prove it," said Beef, "don't you worry."

"I haven't finished yet," went on Wilson. "It's that other thing you said about Rose and me that I'm thinking of. What right you have to come along and make immoral suggestions to us I don't know, but let me tell you this. While we're on the subject of the illustrated Sunday papers, I should say that it's people with minds like yours that write them. Rose and I have been properly married now for nearly a year, and why we didn't tell anybody is nobody's business."

At this point I interrupted. "What *I'd* like to know," I said to Beef, "is what connection this man has with the crime. And what's all this about money?"

"His connection with the crime," said Beef, "is that he's a witness who Inspector Stute may be able to do without, but I can't. He saw that old man leaving the gates that morning, and he was the second on the scene of the murder."

This was disheartening. "So you've come all the way to Ostend after a minor witness?"

Beef looked almost human. "I've come all the way to Ostend," he said, "after a silly young fool who's nearly ruined his life, and may yet be able to put it right if he does what I tell him. How much of that five hundred pounds have you got left?" he asked Wilson.

A broad grin spread over the chauffeur's face. "About seven hundred and twenty," he said.

I thought the Sergeant was working to suppress a smile, but he spoke severely. "Well, I'll tell you what. You come straight back with me and see Mr. Peter Ferrers. If you hand him back the money at once, I don't think he'll say anything more about it. But if you don't, it'll be my duty to have you extricated."

"Extradited," I whispered. Beef scorned to correct himself.

Wilson grinned. "Well, I suppose that's decent of you," he said, "but you might have given me a few days longer here and let me turn it into a thousand."

"Or lose it all," said Beef. "I know you young chaps. What about the years I spent in the Force with nothing happening but a few chickens stolen and a drunk to run in for the night? Do you think I never wanted to hop off and see things? Everyone has that feeling whatever job they're in. But you can't go doing it. Not on stolen money, anyway."

"Who else knows about this?" asked Ed Wilson. "Do the police?"

Beef's chest swelled. "No one knows about it—only me," he said. "It took old Beef, what Inspector Stute doesn't think much of, to realize that there were two lots of five hundred pounds. One of them had been drawn when Benson was away on his holidays, and never paid over at all."

"But what was all this paying of money to Benson by Stewart Ferrers?" I asked impatiently.

"That's one of the things we've got to find out. In the meantime I noticed that the five hundred pounds was locked away in a drawer in Stewart Ferrers's bedroom, whereas the confession of suicide, which would have been equally incriminating, was still in his pocket. How was that? Well, I'll tell you. Because the five hunded pounds that was in his drawer wasn't the same that he'd paid to Benson that night at all, that's why."

"But how did you know?" I asked.

"I didn't *know*," said Beef, "but I knew this young fellow had something up his sleeve. I'm used to dealing with your type, you know," he said to Wilson. "I've had young constables under me just like you. And I could tell there was something you was hiding. Then when you disappeared, I guessed you'd found that wad of notes on Benson in the morning, and slipped them in your pocket."

"How did you trace me here?" asked Wilson with some interest.

"That's part of my method of investigation which I don't intend to reveal," was Beef's grand reply. "And now I should like to know if you're going to be sensible and come back with me?"

Wilson and Rose exchanged glances. I felt there was more than ordinary understanding between these two people, and was inclined to envy them the future.

"Yes," said Wilson, after a moment's hesitation, "I'll come. You think you can put it right with Peter Ferrers, do you?"

"I can't promise you that," said Beef, "but I don't think there's much doubt."

Ed Wilson seemed relieved, but he made no comment beyond a curt promise to be on the night boat.

"Better hand us over the money before you go," said Beef.

"The five hundred, you mean?" asked Wilson anxiously. ·

"What you've been doing here is no business of mine," was Beef's ponderous reply. "I'll return this money to its owner, and you must hope for the best."

Wilson invited us to his hotel, where, he said, he would give us the packet, and the four of us marched into the Super Splendide, a vast building not far from the Casino.

"Doing yourself all right, wasn't you?" said Beef. "Mr. Townsend and I were staying at the Liverpool."

Wilson grinned. "Why not?" he said. "It was only for once in a lifetime, and it was worth it. I know now what its like to live on a decent scale."

Beef shook his head. "You've got to get back to your job," he said severely, "and put all this non-sense out of your head. It'll get you into worse trouble than this if you're not careful. I've seen young chaps ruined by no more than a taste for big cigars." He turned to Rose. "Can't you put some sense into his head?" he said. "You'll have him a criminal before you know where you are, with all this talk about riches and luxury."

Rose spoke for the first time. "I don't think I should mind," she said in a quiet and blasé voice, "as long as he didn't get caught, or anything sordid like that."

Beef made an impatient sound with his lips. "If I thought you meant that," he said, "I wouldn't half have something to say to the pair of you. But I believe this'll be a lesson. Now go and get those notes, and let's get off."

Wilson made an application at the manager's office and returned with a packet similar to the one we had examined at the Cypresses. "It's all there," he said. "When I won last night I returned the full amount. I was going to send it back in any case."

Beef's final comment to me when we were alone on the deck of the steamer going home with Ed and Rose Wilson below was characteristic.

"This roulette must be all right," he said. "Two hundred and twenty pounds in two days. I wish we'd had the time to try it."

Chapter XVIII

Our return to London was a cue for a sudden burst of activity on Beef's part. He told me that we should really have to get down to this, that there had been too much playing around, and that he meant business if no one else did. As Stewart Ferrers would come up for trial in about a fortnight, this resolution seemed reasonable enough, and I asked him if there was anything I could do. I was surprised to hear him say that there was.

"I want you to take Peter Ferrers and Sheila Benson out to dinner tonight. Somewhere classy," he added.

"What about the expense?"

"That's all right," said Beef, "I've got money for expenses."

"Are you suggesting that I should give Peter Ferrers dinner with his own money?" I asked.

"It's not his own money yet," said Beef, "and it won't never be if I can clear Stewart as I expect. You ring him up and ask him, and ask her too. Tell them you've got something to explain about Wilson."

I nodded and went to the telephone. Rather to my surprise, they both accepted—Peter quietly, Sheila with verbal enthusiasm. Beef then gave me my instructions. It was his wish, apparently, to "have a look round" Peter's flat while he wasn't there, and in this design I was expected to assist him. The scheme he evolved for his own entry was ingenious, and really seemed to argue that he was not such a blunderer after all. I was to call for Peter that evening, and tell him that Beef and I had noticed a man in a jeweller's shop not far from his flat whom we suspected of being the mysterious Orpen or Oppenstein. I was to say that Beef urgently wanted the point cleared up, and persuade him, Peter, to go round the corner and, on the pretence of examining something in the window, see if the man really was their visitor of some years ago. While he was out of the building I was to admit Beef into the flat and conceal him somewhere until Peter and I had left. Then, while we were dining, Beef would have all the opportunity he needed for making the search.

"Do you suspect Peter Ferrers, then?" I asked.

"Never mind who I suspect. If you do as I ask you, we'll very soon get to the bottom of this."

Duly, at seven-fifteen, I rang the electric bell at the door of Peter's flat in that large block which he had mentioned to us as his address. He opened the door himself, and seemed quite genial and pleased to see me, perhaps a little relieved that Beef, on this occasion, was not expected to make an appearance. He gave me a drink, and I set about explaining the story of Ed Wilson. He seemed, as usual, more concerned for his brother's sake than for anything else.

"It really does look as though Stewart was being blackmailed," he said. "I can't understand that. However, I've arranged for us all to see him on Thursday, and perhaps that will clear the matter up a bit."

"But about Wilson," I began, for I had taken an interest in the young man and his wife.

"So far as I'm concerned, there's nothing to be said. He's returned the money. By his own account he stole it from Benson, and if, as I feel confident, Stewart can clear up this suggestion of blackmail and say why he was paying the doctor that sum, it's really for Sheila to say what should be done. But I've no doubt that she will think as I do. Very reprehensible of course, but one can understand it. The silly boy had these ideas about seeing the world, and five hundred pounds in small notes belonging to a dead man was too much for him. I think it's rather pathetic that his great adventure should have ended in Ostend, of all places."

"Well, I think that's a very decent way of looking at it, but by the way..." and I began to tell him about Orpen. He was frankly incredulous.

"I don't see how it can be Orpen," he said, "unless he's lost a lot of money. He always seemed a most flourishing individual. Not at all the sort of man you'd expect to find in a small jeweller's shop in the Edgware Road."

"Well, that's what Beef thinks, and you know

that when he gets these ideas into his head they take a lot of shifting. He must have some reason for supposing that it's Orpen. At any rate, it will be easy enough for you to settle the matter either one way or the other; it's only a few hundred yards away, and you could see in a moment if it were he or not."

Peter nodded. "I suppose I shall have to," he said, "but I get a little tired of humouring your old sergeant. Actually I think I've a higher opinion of him as a detective than you have. It may seem odd, but I have the greatest confidence that he will get to the truth about this case. And the truth certainly isn't that my brother's a murderer. But that doesn't make it any easier to put up with what seem the stupidities of his method, and now and again I wish that I had someone more frigidly efficient."

"Still," I persisted, "you'll go round, won't you?"

"Yes, I'll go round," said Peter. "I'll go round straight away. Pour yourself out another drink; I shan't be long."

I waited four minutes after I heard the doors of the lift clang to, then the long whine as it took Peter down to the ground floor, before I ventured out into the passage. But when I did so there was no sign of Beef. From one of the flats along the corridor came a sudden burst of music as a young woman came out pulling on her gloves. Then she closed the door after her and the music ceased. Her high heels tapped icily on the stone as she walked away from me towards the lift at the far end of the passage, and the word or two she said to the cleaner in a baize apron who was gently moving a mop over the polished surface of the floor floated back to me in unrecognizable form. This man's bent and distant figure—for the passages of that block seemed interminable—annoyed me, for it meant that the Sergeant's entry would have a witness. I stood there hesitating, and noticed that the man was moving this way, steadily cleaning as he went. His back was towards me, and it wasn't until he was right outside the door that he said " 'Ush" in a sepulchral voice, and I knew that it was Beef.

"Ridiculous," I told him when we were safely inside Peter's flat. "You risked the whole thing with that nonsense. If you'd come up here normally dressed. . ."

"I did," he said. "I only put this on when I got up to the landing."

"Supposing one of the porters had seen you. What do you think he'd have thought? Whereas if you'd been in your ordinary clothes there would have been nothing to it."

"I had my reasons," said Beef. "Now, where shall I hide?"

It was useless, I reflected, to search one of these modern flats for a cupboard large enough for a man to stand in. The safest place was obviously the kitchen, and this wasn't hard to find. Beef stepped in and sat down while I returned to do as Peter had invited me, and take another drink. It seemed a long time before I heard his latch-key in the door, but when he entered he showed no sign of excitement or dismay.

"Nothing like him," he commented tersely. "I can't think what gave Beef the idea. Orpen was a big man." He glanced at his watch. "Hadn't we better move along," he said, "if we're to meet Sheila at seven-forty-five?"

I agreed very heartily, and was relieved when the two of us had entered the lift, leaving Beef in possession of the flat.

I had chosen the Cul-de-Sac for dinner, though I don't know whether this would have been what Beef had described as "classy." Certainly the cooking is as good there as anywhere in London. But its traditionally dingy walls and tarnished candelabra, the red plush seats preserved from before the war, and its air of having been patronized by Edward VII, might not have seemed to Beef to make it the kind of place that he associated with "society."

Sheila Benson really looked rather fine in a deep green dress which suited her dark eyes and hair. When she and Peter greeted one another it was, I felt, as very close and understanding friends. There was no gush or demonstration, but real pleasure and happiness in seeing one another again.

"This is charming of you, Mr. Townsend," she said, "and I hope we're not going to talk about finger-prints and things all the evening."

I wanted to discourage any of the levity which

had characterized our last conversation, and said, "I'm afraid while Stewart Ferrers is still under arrest we are bound to find ourselves still concerned with this case."

"Naturally," she said, "only don't let's be morbid. Have you, or your old Beef, discovered anything concrete yet?"

I evaded this awkward point by suggesting a drink, and we sat in the little foyer of the restaurant waiting for a table and enjoyed Tio Pepe. For the moment at any rate the details of the case seemed to have been pushed out of the door. There was a warmth and comfort in our casual conversation, as in the smell of cooked food and the subdued sounds of cutlery and careful movement in the other room.

As I watched the two of them I was suddenly struck at the strangeness of the fact that neither of them could be thought to be deeply concerned with the horrible facts which overhung them. To see Peter sipping his sherry and smiling at Sheila, one could never have believed that his brother was to be tried for murder in a fortnight. And to watch Sheila, who made no pretence at all of wearing mourning, was equally incomprehensible. I wondered whether Beef's theory, if he had a theory, took this into account.

We moved into the restaurant and ordered our meal. Once again I noticed how wholeheartedly these two studied the menu, how amiably they discussed with me the matter of wine, how much like a dinner with any engaged couple this seemed. The conversation turned to Wilson, and I repeated to Sheila the story which I had already told Peter Ferrers. She laughed outright.

"Ridiculous boy," she said. "I always rather liked him though. Didn't you, dear?" she added to Peter.

Peter nodded. "Seemed a decent sort of a chap. However, he's returned the money, so there's no great harm done. Beef needs him as a witness, you say?"

I pointed out that one piece of evidence had been supplied by Wilson alone.

"Does Beef depend on that?" asked Peter.

"He never tells me what he's working out until the last."

"But you think he's getting somewhere?"

"I've been driven to the conclusion," I said, "that Beef always gets somewhere in the end. The more I see of that man, the more I'm convinced that what appears to be simplicity is buffoonery as often as not. I sometimes wonder if he doesn't put it on. Some buffoons are extremely acute, you know. Like Touchstone."

"I daresay," said Peter, and became occupied with his food.

As the evening went on, the apparent indifference of these people began to trouble me. I felt oppressed with an odd sense of responsibility. If Stewart were innocent there seemed to be nothing in the world except the ability of Beef which could save him. And who was I to judge how far that

went? I had to admit that I never knew with Beef
how much his success had been luck and how
much a natural gift. And if an innocent man's life
hung on it, it was a distressing position for me.
Perhaps I showed this preoccupation, and perhaps
Peter recognized the cause of it, for when we parted
that evening he left me with a remark that seemed
to me, in retrospect, quite extraordinary. With
calm cheerfulness he patted my shoulder.

"Look here, Townsend," he said, "I shouldn't
worry yourself unduly. I've a strong feeling that
everything's going to be all right. What's more,
Wakefield agrees with me." And with Sheila on his
arm he turned away.

I walked back to my rooms pondering that. Had
he some secret piece of evidence that would clear
his brother, or what did he mean? And why that
sudden reference to Wakefield, whose name had
not occurred in the conversation during the whole
evening?

Chapter XIX

THIS time I was really anxious to hear from Beef what was the result of his search in Peter's flat. It was just the kind of job in which he excelled. Without haste or flurry he would have gone through every nook and cranny in those rooms and, if there was any kind of evidence there, he would have found it. So that it was in good time the following morning that I went round to his small house and found him reading the newspaper.

"Lots of news," he remarked sagaciously.

"Have you?" I said.

"I meant here," he returned, tapping the *Daily Mail*. "Hitler's off again about something. And they've bumped another dozen of them off in Russia."

"I'm more interested," I said, waving aside the fate of Russian reactionaries and German Jews, "in what you discovered last night in Peter's rooms."

"Oh, ah, that," said Beef. "Well, I've got a little surprise for you there. After you'd gone I set to work. There was nothing solid, as you might say, around the room that told me anything. Artistic, mind you. Books and that. I daresay my wife's cousin who's in the antique trade could have learned a thing or two, but I didn't. Then I started on his papers."

"But, Beef," I said, rather angrily, "what right had you to examine Peter's papers? You're employed by him."

"In a case of murder," said Beef ponderously, "you can't stop to consider little things like that. You've got to find the evidence."

"Do you suspect Peter, then?"

"I haven't said that. But sometimes people hold evidence back with the best intentions. Or else because they don't know it is evidence. Anyway, you've got to get at the truth. By fair means or foul. Well, as I was saying, I began to look through his papers. I found a lot of interesting facts, but for a long time there was nothing, as you might say, to go on. There was letters from Sheila Benson that would make your hair stand on end, coming from a married woman. Business letters from his brother, stiff and formal most of them. Nothing to show he'd been philandering around with anyone else, so I daresay this carrying on with Mrs. Benson was genuine enough. Then, right down in one of the lower drawers in his desk, just stuck in a plain envelope, I found this."

Beef fumbled in his pocket-case and withdrew a small slip of paper which he handed to me. On it I read these words: "Add this to the medicine." That was all.

"Well?" I said.

"That's Benson's handwriting," returned Beef.

"What about it?"

"Well, in the first place, don't you think it's rather extraordinary for a doctor to be telling anyone else to *add* something to medicine he's already prescribed? He'd never do such a thing in the ordinary way. If the medicine wasn't right he'd have it dispensed again. Never trust a private person to do that sort of a job. Then again, what was it doing kept so careful in an envelope at the bottom of Peter's desk? Even if it had been a prescription he'd wanted again he wouldn't have kept it more careful than that. Why should he have bothered about five words on a bit of paper?"

"Perhaps he regarded it as evidence," I suggested brightly.

"If so, why didn't he tell me?" returned Beef. "No, there's something very fishy about it, and I'm going to find out what."

"Is that all you discovered last night?"

"That's all there was in his room."

"I hope you put everything back as you found it. I don't want to be involved in any trouble through letting you into the flat."

"Everything's exactly as I found it," returned Beef, "except for this. And if he finds out that this has gone I don't think he'll say anything. When I'd packed it all back and put everything straight I went downstairs to have a chat with the porter. He was a nice fellow; entered for the *News of the World* darts championship last year, but had a bit of bad luck in the second round. Couldn't get the double one. But there you are, it's happened to all of us. I've seen a pair of good players. . ."

"Had he anything to say about the case?" I asked severely.

"Oh yes, I was telling you. We went round to a nice little house at the corner of the mews. A Charringtons' it was. And he told me several things. He was on duty on the night of the murder."

"How did he come to remember that?" I put in sharply.

"Well, stands to reason," said Beef, "he knew Peter Ferrers as a gentleman in the block. Saw the murder had happened at his brother's house. 'Course he remembered everything. Besides, old Stute had checked up on him all right. Trust him. He says Peter came in that evening at about half-past ten. He stopped and asked the porter what had won the three-thirty—him and the porter often having a word about racing. The porter told him and they had a laugh over it because they'd both been on to the same horse. It seems to have been about as good as our Zig-Zag. He said Peter was quite himself, and spoke highly of him. No swank about him or anything like that."

"Did he go out again?" I asked.

"Not by the front door, he didn't. He *could* have gone out by the service lift up till midnight. And there is a fire-escape. But the porter doesn't think either of them likely because how would he have got in again?"

"Surely that would have been easy enough," I suggested. "The porter wasn't on duty all night."

"Well, yes, but I found out something else," said Beef. "The porter told me where he kept his car, and it so happens that he never took that out again. It's an all-night garage, and they remember him bringing it in at twenty-past ten also and saying he wouldn't want it again. It was took up in the lift, stuck at the back of a lot of other cars, and never touched till the following morning."

"These people seem to have remarkable memories for things that happened so long ago."

"You must remember they'd all been questioned at the time by Stute," said Beef.

"Then he couldn't have got down to Sydenham and back again unless he took a taxi?"

"No. And Stute checked up on that. I got on the 'phone to him and asked him. Very rude about it, he was. Asked me if I'd just got to that point. Months ago they found that no taxi had gone down to Sydenham that night from anywhere round where Peter lived, and if he had got down by bus or anything, he could only have got back by a two-hour tram ride, and very likely have to wait two hours for a tram. One of the first things Stute had done was to check up on the conductors on that service, and they were sure Peter hadn't travelled."

"That seems to suggest that Stute started by suspecting Peter."

"Not necessarily," said Beef. "You have to look every way when you're investigating."

"What else did the porter tell you?" I asked.

"Nothing, except that Peter had breakfast brought

up to him next morning, and he was there as large as life."

"So once again, you're not much farther on?"

"I wouldn't say that," said Beef. "I wouldn't say that at all. Anyway, Peter Ferrers is coming along here this morning."

I began to feel that the case was hanging fire altogether. "I think," I said to Beef, "that it's about time you told me your theory, if you've got one."

Beef looked very serious and said quietly, "I haven't got one—not what you might call a theory. Everything's in the air. The only thing I'm quite certain about is that Stewart Ferrers didn't murder Benson."

"You realize, I suppose, that unless you can prove who did do it, you haven't much hope of getting him off?"

"Yes, I know that," said Beef. "It's a worrying case if ever there was one. But we've still got to meet the man himself, and I shouldn't be at all surprised if we got something from him."

At that moment the telephone bell rang. The sound seemed startling in that small, frowsty room, for Beef's home had an air of being closed and divided from the world. One never expected anything to be brought here, or to interrupt the drowsy ugliness of these surroundings. Beef answered it.

"Yes," I heard him say, "Beef speaking." And after a pause, "Good morning, Mr. Wakefield. Yes, Mr. Wakefield. Did he really? You only heard this morning? Well, I don't know whether I ought to say congratulations, Mr. Wakefield.... Oh, I quite understand that. Yes, most interesting. Thank you very much, Mr. Wakefield."

He put the receiver down. "Wakefield," he said, of course.

"What had he got to tell you?"

"Something I never anticipated." And Beef began to drum with his fingers on the table.

"Well?" I prodded. "What is it?"

"When he got to the office this morning he found a letter waiting from Stewart's solicitors. They'd been to see Stewart in gaol yesterday and he'd given them instructions. Wakefield was very high and mighty about it. Didn't seem to like ringing me up at all. You know, spoke as though it was beneath his dignity."

I sighed impatiently. "What instructions?" I asked.

"Why, instructions to pay over to the *Passing Moment* the sum they needed to keep it going."

"It seems that the nearer men get to the gallows, the further they turn to the Left," I remarked caustically.

"I shouldn't say it was that," said Beef.

"Then what do you think? Perhaps Wakefield's the blackmailer, and not Benson at all."

"I didn't like that man," Beef pronounced. "Not in the least, I didn't." And with that I had to be content.

Chapter XX

PETER FERRERS was shown in by Mrs. Beef. "I've arranged the appointment with my brother," he said cheerfuly, and once again I found myself bewildered by this young man's manner. He might have been arranging to take us to a pleasant seaside hotel, rather than to be leading us to the gaol where his brother was held on a charge of murder. I remember thinking that this indifference nullified the porter's evidence about his cheerfulness on the evening of the crime. I was quite prepared to believe that even if he had come straight from the scene of the murder, he would still be able to discuss the winner of the three-thirty. A remarkable person altogether.

"What time are we seeing your brother?" asked Beef.

"I've arranged with Nicholson, that's our solicitor, for us to go and pick him up at eleven o'clock this morning. We can see Stewart at eleven-thirty."

Beef nodded and referred to his notebook. "I've got all my notes handy," he said, "everything I want to ask Stewart Ferrers. I didn't know we should have a solicitor there, though."

"Yes, that's necessary," said Peter. "Well, are you ready?"

We drove to some offices in a street off High Holborn and saw the name Starling and Nicholson on the plate at the door. I was relieved to see that I should not have to produce that onerous form of humour at the expense of solicitors firms' names, and that this one was content with a curt partnership instead of any form of repetition. It might so easily have been Nicholson, Nicholson, Starling, Nicholson & Starling. Nor had we the proverbial long wait, for we were shown almost immediately to the comfortable modern office of Mr. Nicholson himself.

The latter rose to greet us. He was a brisk and determined-looking man, bald, a little rubicund, but quick in movement, snappy in speech. He scarcely glanced at Beef as he shook hands with him, and invited us to sit down. His first words showed exactly what he thought of the whole proceedings.

"You think," he said to Peter Ferrers, "that any object will be served by these gentlemen seeing your brother? It seems to me that matters would be less painful, and perhaps less complicated, if we did not trouble him with too many interviews."

Peter was unruffled. "I've great faith in Sergeant Beef," he said.

Mr. Nicholson slammed a book. "Just as you please, of course. I must say that this case begins to look to me as though our only hope of getting the verdict we want for your brother is to have someone else arrested. If this gentleman can help us, as you believe he can, our problems are solved. How have your investigations gone?" he barked suddenly at Beef.

Beef cleared his throat. "Slow," he said, "very slow."

"Have you any suspicions?" pressed the solicitor.

"Not what you could call suspicions," returned Beef, "but I know he never done it."

"That's not much use, unless you know who did. I understand you chased that chauffeur to Belgium. Didn't that teach you anything?"

"Taught me I'm wasting my time not playing roulette," countered Beef. "Two hundred and twenty pounds in two days he made."

The solicitor turned to Peter again. "I feel bound to advise you against employing this man further," he said curtly. "I don't know why you should think he can be of service, or how he can have acquired any reputation. I say this now while he is present because I think it should be said."

I felt it time I intervened. "My friend Beef does not carry his goods in his shop window," I said quietly.

That might have ended the matter, but unfortunately Beef became truculent and irrepressible.

"What's wrong with my shop window?" he asked. "I never made no claim to being handsome. I'm a detective, not a beauty chorus."

Nicholson stared bleakly at him. "Remarkable," he said. Then once again addressing Peter, "Well, if you have made up your mind, we will go. I do not want to feel that you have the opportunity afterwards of saying that through my advice you neglected some possibility, however remote."

With that he took his hat from a chromium-plated peg, picked up his fountain-pen from his glass-topped desk, and led the way to the street.

"He doesn't seem to have much of an opinion of me," chuckled Beef as we walked through the outer office.

"Do try and behave sensibly," I hissed in his ear. "People will take you for a complete fool if you go on like this."

That sobered him a little, and he scarcely spoke as the car started on its way.

This was the first time that I had ever been brought as near as this to what one might call the realities of crime. All very well to work out intricate theories, but to interview a man in custody, and aleady charged with murder, was another matter. I felt as though I myself was directly involved, and all the flippancy usually associated with even the most gruesome cases in novels immediately left me as I shook hands with Stewart Ferrers.

He was a sallow, thin man, with a drawn, anxious face and prominent dark eyes. They gave his head something of the aspect of primitive sculpture. As though someone had planned the shape of it generously, started to mould a broad forehead and protuberant eyes, and had then grown tired, or found he had not enough clay, so that the chin and neck lapsed into smaller proportions.

Nicholson spoke first. "Mr. Ferrers," he said, "as

you know, your brother has engaged this detective to investigate the matter of Benson's death."

Stewart nodded.

When Peter was about to speak I felt a thrill of curiosity, for I wondered what attitude there would be between these strangely contrasted brothers. I listened carefully. It may have been my imagination, but I was convinced at the time that there was an iciness, a cruelty in the younger one's voice, which I had not heard before.

"I believe," he said, "that Sergeant Beef was the most capable of the private investigators available. Inspector Meredith, Inspector French, Amer Picon, were all busy on other cases which were far too promising or lucrative for them to leave for a matter of this kind which can scarcely run into a second edition. Nor did I feel there was any hope of tempting Lord Simon Plimsoll into a suburb as unfashionable as Sydenham. But Beef, in spite of his oddity of speech and manner, has an excellent record. He has solved two cases which bewildered more experienced investigators, and I believe he will solve this one. He has already, he tells me, found a number of most interesting clues, and it is our hope that before you are brought up for trial, he will have discovered the guilty person."

"Thank you," said Beef. "And now, sir,"—he turned to Stewart—"may I ask you a few questions?"

The curious tautness of Stewart's face seemed to show what he was suffering, but he made no reply beyond a brief nod.

"Perhaps first you could tell us your story of just exactly what happened on that night."

Stewart seemed to look with appeal at his brother and Nicholson. "I have told it so many times," he said.

Nobody spoke, so that it was as if in desperation he began:

"I had asked Benson to dinner about a week before. There was nothing unusual about that since Benson dined at the Cypresses every two months or so. It wasn't until two days later that you rang up, Peter, saying that you and Wakefield had a proposition to put to me, and suggested that evening for your visit. I was delighted, because I do not find Benson alone a very exhilarating companion, and I asked you and Wakefield to make a bachelor dinner-party of it. On the day of the murder I called young Wilson and told him that I wanted to go to the theatre on his day out the following week, and asked him to change his evening. He made no objection to this."

"Why did you ask him about those gears?" asked Beef suddenly.

"I had been offered a Daimler car which, I understood, had pre-selection gears. It seemed to me to be a bargain, and I thought of changing the car I had for it, but I wasn't quite sure whether I should be able to handle those gears as easily as the ones on my present car. It was not until the police raised this point that I even knew that Benson's car also had these gears."

"I was out all that day..."

"Where?" interrupted Beef.

Mr. Nicholson answered for Stewart Ferrers. "Mr. Ferrers has given to the police and to me a complete and detailed account of his movements, to which you may refer if you wish," he said sourly.

"All right. Go on," was Beef's only comment.

"I was out all that day, and returned to the Cypresses only just in time to have a bath and change before dinner."

"Did you go into the library?" asked Beef.

"To the best of my recollection, not at all. Over dinner there was a lively political discussion in which Wakefield distinguished himself by an effective, if somewhat aggressive, statement of his case. He is, as you probably know, what can best be described in my view as an anarchist."

"Bombs and that?"

A very faint suggestion of a smile passed over the weary features of the prisoner. "Perhaps hardly bombs," he admitted, "but destructive methods that are scarcely less dangerous. This paper of his admittedly aims at the downfall of our whole economic system, and of course I could have no sympathy with it. But Wakefield is an eloquent fellow, and his arguments were not without interest. We rose from the table almost reluctantly, and took our coffee in the library. It was here that my brother gave me a book he had brought with him; a fine edition of Omar Khayyám. He knew that I was an admirer of Fitzgerald's remarkable translation.

I remember that I read aloud several of my favourite stanzas."

"Why did you choose that one about the tapster?" asked Beef. "I know a publican often does get a bad name, but I can't think why you should have read that out."

Mr. Nicholson sighed. "Surely," he suggested icily, "Mr. Ferrers's literary preferences at least are his own affair?"

"It was then that my brother and Wakefield put to me their suggestion that I should give financial backing to their paper. I was willing to do what I could for any enterprise of my brother's, but I did not feel, at the time, that my conscience would allow me to support this particular publication. On that matter I have, however, recently changed my mind and decided that I will do what I can for my brother's sake."

"Was there any nastiness about it?" asked Beef.

Stewart seemed remarkably patient in spite of the double strain which was being imposed on him. "Very little was said," he explained. "The request was made, and refused, in a few words. At half-past nine, or thereabouts, my brother and Wakefield said good night and left the house, and I found myself alone with Dr. Benson."

Chapter XXI

BEFORE you go any further," began Beef, "let's hear what you've got to say about this Doctor Benson."

For the first time Stewart Ferrers seemed to have been made uncomfortable by the question. He hesitated a moment, and I noticed that on his large pale forehead there were signs of perspiration.

"Benson had been our doctor for a good many years," he said, "and we had never had any complaint about his professional abilities. There was a suggestion, I believe, that he drank rather more than was good for him, and my friend the Vicar (an excellent fellow, Smyke) disapproved of his advocacy of cremation. But otherwise there was little that could be said against him. I cannot describe him as a close personal friend, but I liked to have him to the house from time to time in common courtesy. But that evening would, in any case, have been the last time I should have invited him."

"Why?" said Beef loudly.

"Because," Stewart explained in his cold, precise voice, "he made a most extraordinary suggestion to me as soon as we were alone. He hinted that there had been some sort of friendship between me and his wife, a lady with whose acquaintance I had scarcely been honoured, and (if I must be frank) whose personality, so far as I understood it, met with my disapproval."

I thought I noticed an exchange of glances between the two brothers which looked anything but friendly to me.

"Why, what was wrong with her?" said Beef.

"I don't think we had better discuss that," said Stewart, "if you don't mind. Suffice it to say that I should not have wished my name to be associated with hers even had she not been a married woman. But Benson claimed to have heard a rumour of a most ridiculous kind which suggested that I had been in her company several times, and I naturally resented the suggestion, and told him so."

"So you had a bit of a row, then?"

"Well, I see no point in concealing the fact. Our argument was certainly acrimonious. To suggest that it led, or could have led, to any sort of violence on my part is, of course, preposterous. But we certainly disagreed "

"Now we come to something, Mr. Ferrers," said Beef, watching the prisoner very closely, "about which I want a straight answer, if you don't mind. Duncan distinctly heard Benson use this sentence, 'It's in my surgery now.' What did he mean by that?"

I think we were all watching Stewart more closely then than at any other time during the interview, for Beef had succeeded in bringing out this question with an air of great importance. I was certain that it embarrassed Stewart Ferrers acutely. He hesitated, then:

"I don't know," he said. "I cannot possibly reconstruct a whole conversation held weeks ago, and remember every phrase that was used in it. It might have referred to anything. I'm sorry I can't help you there."

"But surely you must know what he was talking about," continued Beef. "I mean, even if it was something you'd lent him, you'd know what it was."

"I have told you I don't know," said Stewart, his voice rising to a higher pitch, and Nicholson again interrupted.

"Mr. Ferrers must not be irritated by these senseless inquiries," he said.

"All right," conceded Beef, "only I'd like to remind you that I'm trying to help him. But I've got to ask something else that's going to upset him, I'm afraid." He used the rhetorical pause with deadly effect, and then came out, as if blundering, with the blunt query, "How was it there was arsenic in the whisky that night?"

I was sitting next to Stewart Ferrers, and I am convinced that he was trembling. I thought that if this question really hit him, however, he kept his head remarkably well.

"I have no conception as to what you can possibly mean by that suggestion," he said stiffly.

Nicholson broke in. "What exactly do you mean?" he flashed, as though for the first time he was interested in the activities of Beef.

"I mean what I say. I could smell arsenic in that whisky, and I've got a sample of it at home now."

"Are you suggesting that Benson was poisoned as well as stabbed, then?"

"No," said Beef, "I don't suggest anything of the sort. I just wanted to know if Mr. Ferrers could account for it in any way."

"I certainly cannot," said Stewart Ferrers.

The atmosphere in that little, steam-heated room had grown almost too tense to bear. The bare distempered walls, the varnished furniture and the large radiator were oppressive enough in themselves, but the human element was even more disturbing. The strange attitude of brother to brother, I could not analyse. I was not sure if a blinding hatred was working underneath their cold civility, or if they were joined by some blood-bond which had now triumphed over their petty difficulties. But I was convinced that between them there was something unusual, something outside the range of normal human emotions. Nicholson, who I felt to be a competent lawyer, was plainly bewildered by Beef, and by the suggestion that Beef was making. He seemed to wonder whether to dismiss the Sergeant as a blunderer more likely to bring trouble to his client than help, or whether to take him seriously. I myself, apart from the necessity of remaining a dispassionate observer, was genuinely at sea.

"All right, we'll leave that," said Beef. "What time did he go?"

"I've calculated that as accurately as I can and given the police the result. I should say it was about a quarter-past eleven."

"You parted friendly?"

There was another hesitation. "We were never friendly," said Stewart at last.

"You saw him out, did you?"

"Yes, I went to the front door with him. He'd been expecting his car to be brought around but presumed, I remember, that it must have been taken up to his house. He walked off down the drive, and I shut the door behind him."

"Did you bolt it?" asked Beef.

"No, it is never bolted. The servants have complete freedom outside their working hours, and each has a latch-key. I didn't know who was in and did not think it my business to wonder about that."

"I daresay there's servants in many a house would be glad of that. Then you just left the front door locked with the Yale?"

"That's right."

"How about the doors and windows and things?"

"It was Duncan's place to see to those. I had absolute confidence in Duncan."

"Well, he's gone now," reflected Beef. But this failed to elicit any reaction from Stewart, Peter or Nicholson. "What did you do then?"

"I went to bed," said Stewart.

"Straight away?"

"I turned the light off in the library, and walked straight upstairs."

"There was nothing unusual at all?"

"Absolutely nothing."

"Are you a good sleeper?"

A troubled look crossed Stewart's face. "I haven't been here," he said, "but until this all happened, I have always slept excellently."

"So you dropped off quick, then?"

"As far as I can remember, almost at once."

"Did you wake up in the night?"

"No, my bedroom was at the back of the house, and I slept without interruption until Duncan brought my tea in the morning."

"So that's all you know about that evening?"

"Yes, that's all."

Beef seemed to screw up his eyes. "What was that bit of paper found in your pocket, then, about some Saint and that?"

"I'm simply unable to account for it. I've already told this to Stute. I can only presume that somebody, anxious to incriminate me, had pushed it into my pocket."

"You won't half have a job to make anyone believe that," was Beef's comfortless reflection.

Nicholson squirmed slightly at this, but did not interrupt.

"Then, about that money," said Beef. "There was five hundred pounds in single notes found up in your bedroom. What was they doing there?"

Stewart cleared his throat. "A little eccentricity of mine," he said. "I was very fond of horse-racing, and went in for it on a fairly large scale. My position as a churchwarden made it inadvisable for me to run credit accounts with bookmakers, and I did my betting, cash, through Duncan. I kept these sums for this purpose."

"Yes, but did you know there was another lot found beside Benson's body?"

I was certain this time that Stewart started. "The police never mentioned that."

Beef chuckled. "The police didn't know nothing about it," he said. "It was I and Mr. Townsend what followed a man half-way across Europe. . ."

"To Ostend," I interrupted reprovingly.

"Well, Ostend then," said Beef, "who brought that to light. How do you account for it?"

"I think it must have been in a drawer in my bureau. How it came to be beside Benson, I can't say."

Beef had evidently finished his questions, for he snapped his notebook to and fixed the elastic band round it. "Well, Mr. Ferrers," he said, "I'll do my best. But you make things very difficult, you know. There's a lot more things you could have told me..."

Nicholson rose. "I think we've had enough of this," he said.

"Very well," said Beef, "it won't make no difference to my efforts. But you're leaving me to work in the dark, and work alone."

Stewart seemed to be troubled by some inner doubt. "Perhaps if you came here alone," he said in a very low voice.

"I couldn't allow that," said Nicholson quickly. "I, after all, am responsible for your defence."

Ferrers subsided again, and we left him with his face in his hands.

Chapter XXII

I DON'T know much about these things," said Peter when we were out in the fresh air again, "but it strikes me that if you could find the bookmaker with whom these mysterious bets of my brother's were made, it would be useful evidence for the defence."

"I'd sooner find the murderer," said Beef. "But in the meantime I'm inclined to agree with you. Supposing we hopped down to Sydenham straight away?"

I sighed, for the thought of the faded grandeur of that suburb was not a welcome one to me. But Peter had agreed with a nod, and when we had dropped Nicholson at his office, we once again crossed the river.

For some time we went along in silence, with Beef, who was beside me in the front, casting apprehensive glances at any car which came within three feet of us. I disliked driving with Beef because he did so little justice to my more than average skill with a car in traffic. Suddenly he gave a low moan.

"What's the matter?" I said quickly.

Beef's only reply was a prolonged animal sound. He was leaning forward slightly in the seat, and had one hand thrust between his coat and waistcoat just below the heart.

"It's my stomach," he said at last, "hasn't been the same since we come back from Ostend."

"If you're referring to the food," I said, slightly nettled, "in my opinion it was excellent."

"Still, that's what it was," said Beef. "Foreign cooking what's enough to turn anyone's stomach. You never know what they're giving you when they get it up all fancy like that. Stands to reason there must be something wrong with it when they have to serve it up in disguise, as you might say."

Beef seemed to be ruminating over the subject for some time and his only remark during the next ten minutes was to the effect that he knew what would cure it, and since both Peter and I ignored this hint he lapsed into a sulky silence, and seemed to be performing the difficult task of bringing his mind back to the job. At last he turned to Peter as if he had suddenly remembered something.

"It might be a good idea," he said, "to get that whisky analysed. You remember, what I smelled arsenic in. Do you know of a good analyst I could send it to?"

"Why, as a matter of a fact I do," replied Peter immediately, "a man called Stevenson. I've got the address at home somewhere; I'll send it to you, shall I?"

"Can't you remember it now? " asked Beef impatiently.

Peter could not, but he recalled that the man's initials were W.L. and that Beef would be sure to find it in the 'phone book, with which information, duly entered in his notebook, Beef had to be content.

To our surprise, it was the cook herself who opened the door to us at the Cypresses. "Oh, it's you," she said, referring to Beef rather than to either Peter or me. "Well, don't expect to find things tidy. It's more than I can do, running up and down those stairs till my heart sounds like an electric road-drill. I said I'd stay here till the affair was finished, and stay I will, but I didn't expect to have the whole house on my hands. What with the coming and going ever since that day, and everything being topsy-turvy on account of that girl, I don't know where I am half the time."

"Why, what girl, Mrs. Duncan?" asked Peter. "Do you mean Rose?"

"No, the other one," said Mrs. Duncan. "Not that Rose isn't as bad in some ways, putting on airs just because she went on a bit of a spree abroad. '*Mrs. Wilson* to you,' she says to me only the other day. Anybody would think she'd married a duke by the way she carries on, instead of that good-for-nothing chauffeur who's put ideas into her head that never ought to have been there. At her age too. Work's too good for her now. Mustn't soil her hands, I suppose. Oh no, it's not her I'm talking about."

"Who are you talking about?" asked Beef, somewhat obtusely.

"That other little hussy," said the cook, scarcely taking time to breathe. "Said she'd had enough of the whole affair she did—as if all of us hadn't— and just packed up her things and cleared off. Didn't leave no address neither. Not that anybody

would want to know where *she'd* gone to. Good
riddance to bad rubbish I say."

"Do you mean to say you don't know where she's
gone off to?" asked Beef with concern.

"Well," said Mrs. Duncan, somewhat mollified
by the presence of an interested audience, "she did
say something about going home, I seem to
remember, so I expect you could find her if you
wanted to. Though why anyone should want to
find her I can't imagine," she ended with spirit.

It was impossible to persuade Mrs. Duncan to
enter the library, but at last, after a great deal of of-
coursing and quite-understanding Peter managed
to get her seated at her own table in the kitchen.

"Now, if you remember," said Beef at last when
we were all settled, "you said something last time I
saw you about you and your husband that was
doing a spot of horse-racing."

"And may I ask you why we shouldn't have a
little bit on the horses now and again?" demanded
Mrs. Duncan truculently. "That and the pools are
about the only way a working man and his wife
can turn an honest penny nowadays. You've got
your fox-hunting and all that, why shouldn't we
have a bet sometimes?"

The idea of Beef "having his fox-hunting" was
too much for me, and the smile which this picture
produced brought Mrs. Duncan's indignation down
on my own head.

"Yes, you can smile," she said. "Come down here
trying to do anyone out of the little enough enjoy-

ment she does get out of life. You can smile."

"But, Mrs. Duncan," protested Peter, "Sergeant Beef has nothing against horse-racing. He wasn't trying to stop you from betting; he just wanted some information."

"Well then," said Mrs. Duncan expansively, "what did he want to make all that fuss about it for?"

"I'm surprised at you doing pools, though," said Beef, rather obviously, I thought, trying another line. "Always strike me as being a bit of a take-in, they do. Now with horse-racing, if you do it right, there's a chance to make a bit. How do you usually come out?"

Mrs. Duncan thawed immediately. "Well, on the whole," she said, "I should say about evens. Of course, we used to have a bit of a splash on the Derby—who doesn't? But taking all in all, I should say we might find ourselves up a few shillings at the end of the year. And then again we might be a few shillings down."

"Ah," said Beef understandingly, "and who might your bookmaker be, if you don't mind my asking?"

"To tell you the truth," said Mrs. Duncan, "I don't know his name. Duncan always put the money on through the newsagent's just down the end of the road. But I expect they'd tell you."

"Duncan used to put some money on for Mr. Stewart Ferrers too, didn't he?" continued Beef in what was supposed to be a casual voice.

Mrs. Duncan looked suspicious immediately and gave a quick glance at Peter before she answered.

"Who told you that?" she asked sharply.

"Why, Mr. Ferrers himself, of course."

"Well, since you seem to know—though I thought it was supposed to be a secret—yes, he did."

Beef then turned the conversation to other subjects, and after having heard a lengthy discourse from Mrs. Duncan on the character of her late husband, we left the Cypresses and drove down to the little newsagent's at the bottom of the road. Beef was only gone a few minutes, and returned with a triumphant smile on his face. As we headed north again, towards the address which Beef had obtained from the newsagent, I began to feel that at last the case was beginning to move. It might be quite a small point we were after, but there was satisfaction in it after the mass of unhelpful evidence we seemed to have collected during the last few days.

Once again Peter and I stayed in the car while Beef entered the office of the bookmaker, and we were chatting pleasantly when, after about ten minutes, the Sergeant returned.

"Well, that's that," he said as he reseated himself next to me.

"What did you find out?" asked Peter.

"Those remarkable sums your brother's been throwing away on the horses," said Beef, "don't ever add up to more than three or four pounds in a year, that's what."

"How do you know that?"

"Well, all the bets were registered under Duncan's name, and in the first place it was easy to see that it was mostly in half-crowns and such, which was what Duncan and his wife would want on for themselves. Every now and again there was a bet of ten bob, and once or twice one for a quid, but even if we took all those as being Stewart Ferrers's it doesn't come to more than a fiver at the most."

"That's not very helpful," I commented.

"It's helpful for the prosecution," said Peter soberly. "If he wasn't using the money for betting, what else could it be but blackmail?"

"Don't you jump to conclusions," said Beef slowly. "We haven't got to the bottom of this by a long chalk. There's a lot of things I don't quite understand yet. But it's only a question of time, you'll see."

"I hope so," I muttered, and Beef gave me a hurt look.

We dropped Peter at his flat on the way back to Paddington, but by the time I drew the car into the side of the kerb in Lilac Crescent, Beef seemed to have shaken off his gloom, and it was in his familiar manner that he said:

"Well, you'll come in for a cup of tea now you're here, won't you? Mrs. Beef'll get some for us in two ticks."

I accepted his invitation, and in a short time we were all three seated round the table in his small back room eating the food which Mrs. Beef had prepared for us.

Beef had a habit, which I well knew, of reciting the day's events to his wife every evening when he returned home. This he proceeded to do now while his wife knitted imperturbably at a length of sock, occasionally interrupting Beef's dramatic monologue with such remarks as, "Did he really? Well, don't let your tea get cold, then," or more simply, "Don't talk with your mouth full, dear."

It was while Beef was in the middle of a description of Stewart in gaol that the telephone bell rang, and he stopped in mid-sentence with his mouth slightly open.

"Whoever can that be?" said Mrs. Beef placidly. "I expect it's only a wrong number."

But Beef brushed her remarks aside, and was out in the little hall almost before the bell had rung three times. The muffled sound of his voice came to us through the door, but we could not hear the words. It was quite a lengthy conversation, and when at last Beef returned his face was flushed with exertion and his eyes sparkled.

"Who do you think that was?" he asked pregnantly. "It was that antique-dealer's wife. You know, where we bought the dart-board."

"Dart-board?" I queried. "Oh—where we found the swordstick, you mean."

"That's right," said Beef. "Well, she says she's got on to that old man what sold them the stick. She's followed him round, just like I thought she would, and now all we've got to do is to go down there straight away and see what he's got to say for himself."

Chapter XXIII

Look here, Beef," I said, "I think you'd better go down to Sydenham alone this time. I really don't think I could face that suburb again tonight."

"Now then, none of that," Beef returned, though quite good-humouredly. "You know very well I can't go trapezing down there in buses. Besides, if things turn out as I think they will, I can promise you this will be the last time. What's wrong with Sydenham, anyway?"

"Oh, I daresay it's all right," I conceded, "but I'm tired of it, Beef, and I'm tired of this case. You seem to keep fidgeting about with little bits of evidence, and you don't give me any idea where it's leading."

"Still," said Beef with irrepressible optimism, "you must admit that this is promising. That old chap might be the murderer himself," he chuckled.

"Don't be silly," I snapped. "You may be able to lead other people up all sorts of garden paths of suspicion, but don't try it on me. You know very well you don't think this old man had anything to do with it."

"I shouldn't go so far as to say that," said Beef, "but we'll see what *he* has to say."

"Oh, all right," and once again I got into the

driving seat of my car, and we set out on the familiar road to the south-eastern suburb.

We did not need to enter the shop, for the antique-dealer's wife was standing in the doorway scanning the road as we drove up. Her round eager face was flushed, and a small black hat tottered precariously on her untidy hair. She grasped an umbrella in her hand, and when she saw us drawing up she waved vigorously.

Beef, however, stepped down with leisure and decorum from the car, and brushed his overcoat with his hand before turning to her. "Good evening," he said.

"Oh, I'm so glad you've come," she exploded. "I've been waiting for you nearly an hour. I've got him all right. Found out where his place is, and everything about him. I can tell you his name, and his reputation. I tried to get a photograph of him, but the light was too bad."

"If there's any photographing to be done," said Beef, "I'll arrange for it. All I asked you to do was to find out where the man lived."

"Yes, and I've found out. It was quite by chance, in a way; at least, that was, my seeing him again at all. I went down to do a bit of shopping just after lunch, and at two o'clock, when the public-houses shut, I saw him come rolling out as drunk as you please. I was with another lady, and I turned round to her and said, 'Who's that?' I said. She said, 'That's old Fryer. What about it?' I told her it was a matter of life and death, and set off after him. It took nearly an hour and a half for him to get the little way down to his yard. He kept stopping, and once he sat down on the pavement for half an hour with his head against a lamp-post, until a policeman moved him on. He's known in these parts—well, everybody seems to have heard of him. He's always on the booze, and when he's not he deals in rags and bones and that. They say he's got a lot of money put away, but there's no telling. Anyway, from what I've heard of him, I should say he was capable of anything—even murder."

"Whatever he's capable of," said Beef crushingly, "all I want to see him about is if he's picked up a swordstick which maybe didn't belong to him."

"Well," said the woman, looking at Beef as though she'd been tricked, "I thought this was a *real* crime you were investigating. If I'd have known that's all you was after, I wouldn't have soiled my mind with finding out about a dirty old drunken rag-and-bone man."

"I must say," Beef amended quickly, "that you've been a great help to me. It's the little things what count in a case like this, you know. Now, where did you say this man Fryer lived?"

"You could hardly call it living," said the woman, with a quick return of interest. "He's got a sort of a dirty old yard where he keeps his barrow and things, and sometimes he sleeps there."

"Where else does he sleep, then?" asked Beef.

"From what they tell me, almost anywhere. He's been found in almost every corner you can imagine.

When he's out on the booze, he's likely to stop anywhere and sleep it off. Why, he was even found in the church once. And the times he's been run in for the night, you wouldn't believe."

Beef grunted understandingly. "I've known people like him before," he said.

"But, Beef," I interrupted, "how will you know if this man Fryer is the same man Wilson saw coming out of the front gates of the Cypresses that morning? They might be two different people altogether. And the stick may be just a coincidence."

"I'd thought of that," said Beef calmly. "Before we go along to see him we're going to pick up young Wilson. If we take him along with us he can identify him, can't he?"

Rose and Ed Wilson were living in the little flat over the garage. They both seemed pleased to see us, and as we sat talking for a few minutes I felt that it was genuine enough. In Ed Wilson himself I sensed a change, a certain steadying of character since I had last seen him. He was still self-confident, and as sure of his new plans as he had been of his old. But there was something less selfish about him now.

"We've been talking it over, haven't we, Rose?" he said. "You were awfully decent about that Ostend business, Sergeant. We've put almost all of that two hundred and twenty pounds in the bank. It's going to come in useful."

"*Almost* all of it?" queried Beef severely.

Rose made a grimace at him. "We had a bit of an

outing the other night," she said, "but we only spent a pound or two, honest."

The antique-dealer's wife, who had been sitting in a rather foreboding silence on the settee all this time, now rose to her feet. "I thought," she said icily, "that we were going to capture a criminal. I must say this seems a very strange way of doing it."

Hurriedly Beef told Ed Wilson what had brought us to see him, and Wilson agreed immediately to come with us and see the old man. At the last minute Rose, who refused to be left behind, had to be squeezed into the back of the car, and then, with the antique-dealer's wife sitting somewhat grimly forward on the edge of her seat in order to direct me, we started off again.

The yard in which Fryer lived had at one time been a fairly large mews, but though it may once have housed horses, it had progressed no further, and was now dark and disused, except for the casual occupation of the old man whose headquarters it was. I drew the car a little way past its entrance and we got out and walked back.

"That's it," said the woman. "And that's where he sleeps," she added, pointing with her umbrella to the far end of the yard, where a door hung permanently open on one hinge.

The only light at the entrance showed a cobbled yard some twenty yards long. On either side the entrances to the stables were dark as caves. With the exception of the one at the end of the yard, all the doors had long since been taken away or simply fallen to pieces on their hinges, and the heaps of junk stacked on every available space of the yard increased the effect of some prehistoric cave-dwelling with the kitchen-midden at each entrance. Dirty trodden straw which had spilled over from the packing-cases lay in wet smelling patches, and a dark trickle of rich brown liquid ran down the centre-way of the court.

Rose gave a shudder and drew closer to her husband. "Have we got to go down there?" she asked.

Beef peered down the yard without answering. "Are you sure he's here?" he asked the antique-dealer's wife at last. "Doesn't look like it to me."

The woman nodded vigorously. "This is the place," she said decisively; "I followed him to this very spot. I didn't think it was safe to go any farther, but I watched him as he went into that door at the end. That's where he sleeps, they told me."

Gingerly we began to move forward, following Beef, who was looking cautiously behind each heap of rubbish before taking another step. Every now and again there would be a hurried rustling on either side of us, and then an abrupt silence until we moved again. Strangely enough, the least perturbed of us was the antique-dealer's wife herself. There was a gleam in her eye as she walked forward, keeping close behind Beef. In one hand she clutched her umbrella determinedly, the other held a handful of coat and skirt closely against her as if there were a danger of them falling off.

Nearly half-way down the yard rose a huge

mountain of junk, each succeeding piece having been stacked precariously on the last until it resembled a rough and dilapidated sphinx-like figure. The light behind us gleamed on twisted pipes, old carpets, wheels, and numerous fat porcelain shapes.

Beef began to negotiate it carefully, when suddenly he stopped and held up his hand. At the base of the heap we saw a slight movement, and then with slow dignity a lean black cat walked out into the light. Unable to run from sheer inanition, it stood back and unblinkingly watched us file past as quickly as we could. We stopped in a relatively open space in the center of the yard waiting for Beef to make the next move. He was breathing noisily, and took out his handkerchief to wipe his face.

"I think we might try calling him, don't you?" he said in a hoarse whisper. Nobody answered him, but I think I nodded.

"Mr. Fryer," he called. "Mr. Fryer." There was no answer. Beef looked at us in bewilderment.

"If he's still as drunk as what he was," said the woman, "he won't never hear you."

Beef called again, and this time there was the sound of movement from the end of the yard. The dilapidated door shook slightly as if someone had leaned against it for a moment, and then the figure of a man emerged and stood blinking at the dim light from under his tangled eyebrows before he began to shuffle slowly towards us.

I had never seen anybody who had so completely abdicated the bearing and appearance of a human being as this man. It was not that he looked inhuman in any Frankenstein way but rather that he seemed to have assumed so many of the properties of inanimate matter. He might have been an old tree-stump which, after having rotted comfortably in a swamp for many years, had been stood on end and clothed in a strange medley of coats and trousers in pure parody of a man. Now he wandered slowly towards us with uneven and uncontrolled steps, fumbling with one bony hand in the recesses of his tattered jacket, and mumbling continually to himself all the time.

Beef turned to Ed Wilson. "Well?" he said. "Do you recognize him?"

Ed Wilson did not need to take another look at the man. "That's him," he said confidently.

Chapter XXIV

"Is your name Fryer?" asked Beef.

The old man gave a non-committal grunt.

"I want to ask you some questions in connection with the Sydenham murder." Beef brought out the words as though he were enunciating a death sentence, but they had little or no effect on the person to whom they were directed. The old man continued to stare placidly into Beef's face.

"On the morning after that murder you were seen to leave the garden of the Cypresses carrying a walking-stick. Later on you sold that stick in a local second-hand shop for seven shillings and sixpence. What's more, here it is," ended Beef, pulling from behind him his treasured weapon and displaying it to the old man's indifferent gaze.

There was a long silence, then Beef, growing irritated, said, "Well, what have you got to say for yourself?"

When the old man did speak it was disappointing. "How much do you want for it?" he asked.

Beef grew irate. "I'm not trying to sell it to you," he said.

"Oh, I thought you had something to sell," mumbled the old man.

Beef turned to the antique-dealer's wife. "Is he dippy?" he asked.

Her reply was made in a hoarse whisper. "I don't know, I'm sure. Perhaps there's method in his madness. He looks cunning enough."

Whatever cunning the old man may have had seemed to me to be concentrated in the buying and selling of junk. His only interest in the swordstick was a commercial one. Beef pulled the blade out. "Have you ever seen this before?" he asked.

"When I was with Lord Roberts," began the old fellow, and his voice trailed away into a murmur in which was audible such words as "Bloomfontein" and "De Wet."

"They say he's never been out of London," said the antique-dealer's wife. "He's always talking about foreign places. He gets them off the wireless."

Beef seemed certain that bullying was the best method. "Now then,' he said, "that's enough of that. You tell us the truth. What were you doing in the garden of the Cypresses that morning?"

"I was out in the Klondike," said Mr. Fryer calmly.

Beef looked round with exasperation, then tried a new method. "Look here," he said, "I shouldn't be surprised if we was to buy you a pint or two if you was to tell us anything." It needed an optimist to perceive any greater animation in the old face, even on this suggestion. "Where did you get this stick?"

"I'll give you a shilling for it," the old man volunteered.

"Try taking him down to the pub," said Ed Wilson.

Nobody had any serious objections to the scheme, and the old man himself started walking steadily towards the roadway.

"Don't you think you ought to have a look round this yard?" I suggested to Beef. "Surely there might be further evidence."

Beef shook his head impatiently as he turned to follow Mr. Fryer, and I realized that I might have known that after Wilson had made that suggestion Beef would not delay, even if by doing so he might help his investigations. Or was Beef, I wondered cynically, a sort of modern Drake who could both finish his game of darts and arrest the criminal.

We indicated to Mr. Fryer that he should get into the car, but he slowly shook his head. "Wallama-loo," was all he said, or all we could hear of his next sentence as he moved off along the pavement. And the best we could do was to drive slowly near the kerb, keeping him in sight.

The antique-dealer's wife was in ecstasies. "Isn't it thrilling?' she said, nudging me altogether too vigorously. "I never thought I'd be sitting in a high-powered car chasing a criminal."

"You ought to have met Beef before," I said; "you've got so much in common." On which the Sergeant gave me a reproving glance and Ed Wilson smiled. We must have made an extraordinary quintette driving along there; Rose looking rather frail and silent but quite happy with her husband's arm lightly around her shoulders, the antique-dealer's wife flushed and shining with enthusiasm, Beef solemn and thoughtful, and I incongruously conducting the whole *ménage*.

To our surprise the old man passed the doors of one public-house and walked some hundreds of yards on to another. But my interest was rekindled when I perceived that it was the one kept by the ex-gardener of the Ferrers; the man we had tentatively identified with Omar Khayyám's "surly tapster."

"Now," said Beef, when we were all settled with our drinks, "tell us what you remember about that night."

Old Fryer stared at his glass without answering for a minute or so, then he looked up and I thought there was a more intelligent look in his rheumy eyes. "It was dark," he said, and then stopped.

"Here," said Beef, "have another. Now, what were you saying? It was dark, and then what?"

The old man mumbled to himself for a while and I couldn't catch any of it until suddenly he said, "Like walking in a dream. Went on for days it seemed, then suddenly I saw a light, and made for it." There were more mumblings until he fell silent again.

"Did you reach it?" I asked.

"I just stood there looking," said Fryer, with a puzzled expression on his face, "and I saw..." He paused again, and then his face cleared, and he went on quickly, "And there was Lord Roberts.

'I've got great news for you,' he said..."

"We shan't never get nothing out of him," said Beef despondently. "What sort of a figure would he cut in the witness-box, anyway?"

"How do you know he's not just tricking you?" asked the antique-dealer's wife. "I wouldn't mind betting he knows all about the murder and he's been paid to keep quiet about it. Why don't you answer the Sergeant properly?" she said, suddenly turning on the old man and prodding him sharply with the ferrule of her umbrella.

The old man lurched to his feet with a horrified look on his face. "The Matabele have surrounded the stockade," he shouted, and then sank back on to the form and closed his eyes.

"No, that's no use," said Beef. "I've got to think, I have. Do you play darts?" he said sullenly to Ed Wilson. "Of course you do. Well, come on then. I always think better when I'm playing darts. You'd better sit by old Fryer," he said to me, "just in case he does say anything that might come in useful."

I did not think much of the arrangement, which I took to be merely a manoeuvre on Beef's part to get to the dart-board, but nevertheless I did what he told me. For a time I continued to prod him with short questions, but he only carried on a continuous mumbling to himself as he absorbed the beers I brought him. When I noticed Rose looking amusedly at me I gave up the attempt altogether.

"What do you expect to get out of him, anyway?" she asked.

I explained that as far as we could guess he had been in the summer-house of the Cypresses on the night of the murder and that it was quite possible that he had seen something which would be considered as evidence. In any case we wanted to find out if he had actually picked up the swordstick in the grounds of the Cypresses, or if he had had it with him when he went in there.

"But where does the swordstick come in?" asked Rose. "Doctor Benson was stabbed with that knife, wasn't he?"

"You'd better ask Beef about that," I said. But Beef was concentrating on the double seven in what looked like a losing game, so she did not interrupt him.

"Do you think Mr. Stewart did it?" she asked me; "I don't. Not with a knife he wouldn't have done. He wasn't that sort of a man. Of course he was a cold sort of man, you didn't ever know what he was thinking. But I don't think he could have done a thing like that."

"But there's no special sort of man who is a murderer," I said. "It's something anyone might do without knowing they were going to."

"I didn't mean that I didn't think he was a murderer," said Rose sanely; "I haven't ever seen a murderer, so I wouldn't know. What I meant was that he couldn't have killed Doctor Benson with that knife. He just couldn't have."

Our conversation was interrupted by Beef, who had apparently lost the game to Wilson. "I don't know," he said disgustedly, "I don't seem to be able to do either. My darts game's all gone to pieces, and I can't think what to do next."

"What about taking old Fryer down to the Cypresses?" suggested Ed Wilson helpfully.

"What good would that do?"

"Why, you know, might remind him and all that. We could take him into the summer-house and see what he'd do."

We had some difficulty persuading Fryer to leave with us, for he was by now in no condition to be trusted to his own legs. In the end we walked on either side of him as supports. The car had to be left outside the public-house, but it was no great distance to the Cypresses, so that in a few minutes we were standing on the lawn before the summer-house.

"All right," said Beef, "let go of his arm and let's see what he does."

As far as I could see, the plan succeeded splendidly, for as soon as we had released Fryer's arms he stumbled straight into the summer-house and made for the far corner. There he slumped down on a heap of old sacks and went straight to sleep, refusing to wake up however much we shook or shouted at him.

"Well, that's that," said Beef; "I suppose we shall have to leave him there now. Anyway, we shan't get anything more out of him."

Ed Wilson promised to see to him in the morning, and at that we had to leave it. Rose and Ed Wilson went back to their flat over the garage, and the antique-dealer's wife left us in a more dampened mood than that of half an hour before. Beef and I walked slowly down the drive and out into the road in silence.

"Well," said Beef at last when we had almost reached the car, "I've finished my investigations. I know all I ever shall know about this case."

"Then you know who did the murder?" I asked quickly.

Beef thought for a minute as if arranging his thoughts. "I am not in a position to say who done it," he said at last, "but I know who hasn't done it."

I was disappointed, and said rather slyly, "You'll have to convince Sir William Petterie of that, then. They've got a meeting at the solicitor's office tomorrow to decide whether they're going to use your evidence or not."

"No need for you to worry about that," said Beef with dignity, "I've got my notes."

Chapter XXV

T HE next day was, perhaps, the blackest in my association with Beef. I had known all along that the real test of the value of his investigations would come when he had to convince Sir William Petterie, Stewart's counsel, that he would be worth while as a witness. I knew Sir William's reputation; a great humanitarian, but a shrewd one; and I knew that no bluff would be much use here.

Sir William was a fine lawyer, immensely eloquent and persuasive, but at the same time a man to whom facts were everything. Useless to go to him with vague, tumbledown theories of who might have done this thing—the only revelation that would make much impression on him was either a clear-cut case against someone else, or a definitive reason why it could not have been Stewart.

Beef, it seemed to me, had fumbled clumsily with a great deal of evidence, had chased a number of red herrings, and although he had brought certain matters to light which were apparently unknown to the police, I did not believe before the interview that he would be able to cut much of a figure. In that I suppose I was wrong, although my preconceptions were not unfounded.

I called for Beef as usual after breakfast, and we set off for Sir William's chambers, where we were to meet Nicholson and Peter. Beef was silent during the journey, his face set in lines that might almost have been described as grim. I did not encourage him to talk, for I wanted him to have all the opportunity possible to think out his case.

We were shown into the chambers, and found it a large comfortable room with deep chairs and mahogany book-shelves, in which seemed to cling a faint atmosphere of other conferences. Nicholson and Peter were already there, and Sir William rose to greet the Sergeant. His manner was friendly, and I wondered at first if there was irony in the consideration he showed to Beef, for I had become accustomed to seeing my old friend treated as something of an amiable buffoon. But I soon realized that this lawyer regarded Beef with genuine interest.

He was a tall, handsome man, in his late fifties, with thick white hair, almost boyish in its straightness and cut such as is more usual in elderly Americans than in Englishmen. He had clear straight features, shrewd honest eyes, and the figure of an athlete. He was wearing plus-fours, for it was a Saturday and he had only come up to his chambers for this conference before playing golf. Peter introduced us without explanations, and Sir William invited us to sit down.

"I've heard a great deal about you, Sergeant," he said, "and I'm very anxious to know your views of this case."

"Thank you, sir," said Beef quietly. "I'm afraid you may find them a bit disappointing. I haven't anything really what you might call final to tell you, but I've found out a good deal and I hope it may be of some use."

"Splendid," said Sir William, offering Beef a cigarette, which he accepted. "I've studied the whole thing pretty closely and I have gathered the police's case. I think I should tell you at once that I regard it as a very strong one, though circumstantial at times."

Beef nodded. "So do I, sir," he said. "Uncomfortably strong. In fact I've realized from the very first that the only thing that would break it for certain would be finding out who did murder Doctor Benson."

"You're perfectly sure, then, that Stewart Ferrers didn't?"

"Yes, sir, I'm perfectly sure of that."

"Well, let's have your reasons."

Beef smiled. "I can't exactly put my case in that way, sir. I can tell you what I discovered, but I don't know how much of it can be considered reasons for thinking Stewart innocent."

"Very well," said Sir William, "tell us what you have discovered."

"First of all the whisky that was left standing on the table in the library. As soon as I saw that there I had a sniff at it. I took a sample and I've just had it analysed. By the way," he said, turning aside to Peter, "I must thank you for that analyst's address.

I went to see him, and he did it most satisfactory. Most satisfactory. That whisky contained arsenic."

"But—" began Nicholson, leaning forward from his chair.

Beef held up his massive hand. "I know what you're going to say," he admonished. "You think that only makes the case worse. Well, you may be right. All I can say definitely about it is that someone in that house was trying to poison someone else. Since the whisky was produced only after Mr. Peter Ferrers and Mr. Wakefield had gone, you might guess that they weren't the intended victims, but even of that you couldn't be certain. There are half a dozen people who might have put it in, and half a dozen who might have been meant to drink it. Wilson, Duncan, Mrs. Duncan, Rose, Freda, Mr. Stewart, Mr. Peter, Mr. Wakefield, Doctor Benson, any of those could in fact have poisoned that whisky, and it might have been intended, if circumstances had gone any other way, for Mr. Stewart, Doctor Benson, Mr. Peter, Mr. Wakefield, and Duncan himself, or even Mrs. Duncan if she liked a nip before she went to bed. So that that doesn't help us much. I can only say that the whisky was poisoned."

Sir William was listening intently. "You say that the police never knew this?" he said.

"No, sir. I found that out by myself. You see, it's like this. When the police are investigating a death by stabbing they don't look for poison. Just as in that last case of mine they were trying to find out who'd been murdered, and they never stopped to think who'd done the murder."

"That's interesting," said Sir William, "and certainly a feather in your cap, Sergeant."

"Then there was that bloodstain on the cushion in the library. Someone had run a blade through it to clean it on that. I can't see how that can come into the police's case. If, as they maintain, Stewart had picked up that knife, stabbed Doctor Benson in the throat, and put the knife down on the table again where it was found with the bloodstains on it, what did he stop to clean it for? And did he stick it in twice? It doesn't make sense in accordance with their theories."

"But how do you account for it?" asked Sir William.

"I can't exactly account for it," admitted Beef, "but there's circumstances which we come to in a minute which might help to account for it."

Nicholson gave a loud, exasperated sigh.

"Then again, these rumours about Stewart Ferrers and Sheila Benson. I tried to trace those to their source, but they don't seem to have a source. Everybody's heard them, everybody's repeated them, but nobody, as far as I could make out, had any grounds for them. Benson and his wife had agreed to separate. There seemed to be a perfectly good understanding between them on this point. But the reason for their separation, as Mr. Peter will admit, wasn't anything there was between Mrs. Benson and Stewart Ferrers."

"I'm engaged to Sheila Benson," put in Peter quietly.

Sir William nodded. "How do you account for the rumour, then?" he asked Beef.

"Someone put things about," Beef replied, "and I shouldn't put it past that Vicar. He looked the talking sort to me."

I felt it was time to put a check on Beef's eloquence in this direction. "My friend Beef," I said, "has a quite unreasonable prejudice against the clergy. He never seems to recognize the sterling qualities which many of our hard-working parsons possess, and only sees in them gossip-mongers, spoil-sports, and enemies of Sunday darts."

Sir William smiled gently. "Perhaps we have some of our tastes in common, Sergeant," he said amiably.

"But seriously, sir," said Beef, returning from such remote trivialities as the Church of England to matters more immediate, "I believe these rumours were fabricated. But I believe it was done deliberately by someone who wished to involve Mr. Stewart Ferrers. I ask you to consider this. If it was going to be made to look as though he had murdered Benson, there would have to have been some motive for it, and what could be more handy?"

"What, indeed?" remarked Sir William good-humouredly.

"Then we come to Duncan," said Beef. "Why should he have hanged himself? Nobody's been able to answer me that. It takes something to make an old fellow hang himself, you know, even when he had got a wife like that. You'd be surprised how people cling on to life. . ."

"I shouldn't," said Sir William.

"No, well, of course you know," admitted Beef, "it's supposed he knew too much. But what did he know that was so horrible as to make him string himself up? He'd been with the family, and seemed to have been devoted to them. There's more in that than meets the eye."

"Yes," said Nicholson impatiently, "but how can it help our case? If he knew anything in favour of Stewart the assumption is that he would have wished to have given evidence. The more you emphasize this point, the more you make it look as though he knew something against Stewart."

"Ad-mitted," said Beef grandly, "ad-mitted. But I'm just putting forward these little things that the police don't seem to have taken account of."

"Then there's a lot of funny business over money," he went on. "Look for the woman is supposed to be the way to get at the truth of things. Only they always say that in French. Look for the money when you're dealing with English people. Stewart seems to have been an extraordinary man where money was concerned. We know he was in the hands of a moneylender once. . . ."

"Pardon me," said Nicholson tartly, "we know nothing of the sort. We know that a man who lent money was once a visitor at the house."

"Well, all right. But we do know that he had

these sums of five hundred pounds in one-pound notes about the place. Whatever would a man want those for? He says it was for horse-racing, but I've successfully exploded that theory. The police say he was being blackmailed by Benson, but there's no proof of that. He may have been blackmailed by half a dozen people."

"What about that curious receipt?" asked Sir William.

"Yes, well, that does look bad," admitted Beef, "but how do we know that Benson didn't really mean to commit suicide? It's not final, you know. That's where Stewart Ferrers is silly. He won't speak up about this money."

"What Mr. Ferrers is prepared to tell you, and what he is prepared to tell his solicitors, may be two different things," said Nicholson stiffly.

"I daresay," said Beef, "but it's not the way to help an investigator."

"Investigator!" snapped the solicitor.

But Sir William intervened. "I think Sergeant Beef has already given proof of his energy and ability." he said blandly, "even if he hasn't made our position much easier."

"Thank you, sir," said Beef again, "but that's not all. There's Freda."

"Freda?" repeated Sir William

"Yes, the second housemaid. A noisy little piece, if ever there was one. But she told me something most interesting." And Beef proceeded to outline Freda's story of the stranger in the drive.

"That's extremely good," said Sir William; "that is of real material assistance to us. We must certainly call this girl, and the mechanic. What do you say, Mr. Nicholson?"

"Yes," agreed Nicholson grudgingly, "that is constructive, though of course a little contradictory. So far Sergeant Beef has seemed to infer that this murder was done by someone inside the house other than Stewart. Now his evidence is suggesting that it was someone outside."

"I'm not suggesting anything," said Beef. "I've told you I can't make out who'd done it. It's one of these cases where you've got two and two, and can't put them together. But there you are. There was someone in the bushes that night, and what's more there's further evidence of it. What about this?" he asked. And delving into his pocket he pulled out the latch-key which Ed Wilson had found in the shrubbery that morning. "How did this come to be lying about in the garden? All the locking and bolting that Duncan did doesn't make any difference to the case against Mr. Ferrers while someone else had a latch-key to walk straight in with. That someone else may have been the man Freda saw walking up the drive, it may have been the man who slept in the summerhouse. . ."

"Or it may have been almost anyone," added Sir William; "but the point is that an outsider could have, and possibly did, enter the house that evening."

"Exactly, sir," said Beef; "there you have it. But I think that my most important piece of evidence concerns this swordstick," he continued, brandishing the weapon which he had purchased from the second-hand shop. "But again I've got to tell you that I can't get anything definite out of it. It may mean everything, or nothing, and I don't believe that we shall ever know. I found it in a shop in Sydenham during my investigations, and when I inquired how that shop had come by it they said that they had bought it from an old tramp on what turned out to be the morning after the murder. With a great deal of trouble and some expense I've been able to trace that old tramp." Beef leaned back in his chair, folded his hands over his stomach, and looked from Sir William Petterie to Nicholson as though he expected to be congratulated.

"He is the most disreputable old man," he continued, "and sleeps in a place which, if I was still in the Service, I should never have allowed. But policemen aren't as smart as they were, and sanitary inspectors don't see everything. Unfortunately, when I came to interview this individual, I was unable to extract any information at all. He mumbles a lot of nonsense about foreign places, but whether he does that to make you think he's dippy, or whether he really is a bit simple, nobody in the district seems to be able to say. But what we do know about him is that Ed Wilson saw him coming out of the drive of the Cypresses early the following morning, carrying a stick. Now I have reason to suppose that someone has slept in that summerhouse recently. . . ."

"What reason?" said Nicholson.

Beef pulled out his pocket-case and presently showed us, between his wide fingers, the little pieces of charred paper which he had recovered from the floor of the summer-house when we searched it. "These," he said. "You know what they are? Pieces off fag-ends what somebody's used for a pipe. Now let's suppose that this old bird went to the summer-house that evening and slept there, found the swordstick, and walked out the following morning with it over his arm."

"Exactly," said Sir William. "Let's suppose that. How does that connect him with the crime? Is there any reason to think that he was connected?"

"Well, it seems a bit funny," said Beef. "A man is stabbed to death, and on the morning after an old man what's been hanging round the house all night walks out with a swordstick in his hand. It's a bit of a coincidence, as you might say," and he shook his head warningly.

"But if, as you suggest, he had some connection with the crime," put in Nicholson, "do you suppose he would have stayed on the scene of it for the rest of the night, and walked away in broad daylight? And if he'd used that stick to commit a murder with, would he have sold it in a local shop?"

"I didn't say he'd done it," pointed out Beef, "but I don't think it was all just by chance that he was there."

"Do you think that stick was used at all in the murder?"

"Well, there's that stain on the cushion," said Beef.

"Yes," said Sir William, "there is that."

"Now there's only one more point I want to make," said Beef, "and that's that sentence that Duncan overheard: 'It's in my surgery now.' When I asked Stewart Ferrers about that he said he couldn't remember its being said, and couldn't think what it could have been about. Now when a man's on trial for his life his wits are pretty wide awake. If that sentence had just referred to a book he'd lent Benson, or anything of that sort, it's ten to one he could have given some explanation. But I thought, by the way he said it, that he knew very well what Benson was talking about and just wasn't going to admit it."

"What do you suppose it was?" asked Sir William.

"Ah, there you've got me," said Beef. "When the man you're trying to clear won't tell you what he knows, you can't get very far, can you? Well, gentlemen, that's all I've been able to find out, and I can't piece it together to find anyone guilty."

"I see," said Sir William, turning a ring slowly on his finger. Then suddenly the lawyer looked up. "I don't think we shall need to call you, Sergeant," he said briskly, "though you've given us some important evidence. I shall get Mr. Nicholson to get in touch with that girl, and have the mechanic's evidence clear. I'm afraid there won't be much point in producing this swordstick, or referring to the matter of the poisoned whisky."

"How will you go about getting him off, then?" asked Beef ingenuously.

Nicholson came primly to the rescue. "It's not usual for an investigator employed in a case like this to question the counsel on the methods he proposes to use," he explained, and Beef subsided.

"I'm sorry I haven't been able to do any better," he said, "but there you are," and he reached for his bowler hat.

"You've done very well," said Sir William, and shook hands warmly. But I felt that he was the only man in the room who thought this. I myself was dismally disappointed in Beef, and blamed myself for having an almost superstitious faith in his abilities. When we were out in the open air, I tried to put this to him.

"You realize, I suppose, that if Stewart Ferrers is found guilty, not only will you have failed to save an innocent man, but have ruined you own reputation for ever?"

Beef seemed oddly stoical—even indifferent. "Can't help that," he said. "I done my best."

"Why didn't you produce that bit of paper which you found in Peter Ferrer's bedroom?"

"Well, I couldn't do that," he replied, "not after searching in there without permission, could I?"

"Why so scrupulous? You thought yourself justified in going through his things."

"Well, but it doesn't mean anything, does it?" said Beef, reasonably enough. "If it was something that would help to get Stewart Ferrers off, that would be different. But I don't know where it fits into this case—if it fits in at all."

I tried to rally him. "It isn't like you, Beef," I said. "Your methods may have been unorthodox, but you always seem to get your man."

"I need a drink," said Beef irritably, and he led the way into a public bar.

Chapter XXVI

THE trial of Stewart Ferrers for the murder of Dr. Benson did not arouse the last ecstasy of public opinion. Its headlines, unlike those of many other murder cases, were no larger than those which announced a new war in the East, or a battle in Spain. But it was taken seriously enough for the evening papers to give whole pages of type to the evidence.

The Court, of course, was crowded, and when I looked at the faces in the spectators' gallery it seemed to me that nothing but boredom could have brought all those people together, waiting, neither patient nor impatient, in their seats. Neither relatives nor acquaintances, they had come to watch the slow mental torture of the prisoner in the dock, though to them the whole case was unreal and novelettish, as if the characters involved were no more than cardboard cut-outs designed from the latest thriller. I had expected an avid, even bloodthirsty, interest to be obvious on each face. I had expected to see signs of carefully nursed cruelty in the way this woman leaned forward in her seat. But there was nothing of the sort to be seen anywhere. There was a low hum of voices such as a crowd of people make when they talk desultorily about their gardens or the weather, and no more interest in each succeeding witness, after the case had started, than they would have shown if each were a little twisted piece of wood that fitted somewhere in a puzzle. They could feel neither pity nor pleasure for the fate of the people involved, for to them they were not real people. It passed away an hour or so.

Beef and I had been given seats, and intended to witness the whole case. I was not very comfortable about it, feeling that too many people knew about Beef's unsuccessful part in the matter, and my own association with him. I still had some hope that during the evidence an idea might occur to him which, before it was too late, might even yet enable him to suggest an arrest. But he himself seemed surly and almost inattentive.

When Stewart was eventually brought in there was the usual noticeable hush over the court, and I myself was stangely disturbed. When I had last seen Stewart in prison he had been drawn and worried, but he had given me the impression that it was his innocence and a complete bewilderment at the police's case which had caused it. Now as I watched him enter the Court I felt for the first time in the case the possibility that Beef's assurance might be misplaced. Stewart seemed to be quite unaware of the hundreds of eyes which were fixed on him, although it was obvious that he was nervous to a degree of hysteria. The dark shadows under his eyes made them look unnaturally large even though he kept them cast down as though to ward off, until the last possible moment, the sight of those come to try him. But somehow, and it is difficult to say quite why, I felt that in his actions he was moving as only a guilty man would move. There seemed to be neither defiance nor hope in him.

The case was to be tried by Mr. Justice Seebright, whose reputation I already knew. He belonged to a class of judges which the newspapers have greatly popularized, and one with which I found myself in little sympathy. By posing as unworldly, living in a rarefied atmosphere untouched by the normal trivialities of life, they were able to bring out questions of unbelievably simple ingenuousness to the immense and satisfying laughter from the body of the Court. I could not tell whether Mr. Justice Seebright would indulge his exhibitionism in this way during this particular case, but I hoped, for the sake of the man on trial, that he would not. I may be conservative in feeling that it is bad taste to joke a man's life away, but I felt that Stewart was in no condition to be made part of a music-hall turn.

There was, however, another side to this man which had been little publicized by the press, and that was a wide and observant knowledge of human psychology. However objective a judge should be, it is not possible for him to be a completely passionless cypher, and previous cases which I had read showed Mr. Justice Seebright as being more concerned with the human application of the law rather than an automatic servility to its precise letter.

I do not feel that any purpose would be served by my writing here the long and painful story of those proceedings. They can be found in any newspaper of the time, and except at certain moments there was nothing in them which would seem to have helped Beef to establish the prisoner's innocence, or me to persuade myself (for it had come to that) that Stewart had, in fact, not murdered Dr. Benson.

I remember the prosecuting counsel, Harris Fitz-Allen, whose narrow bespectacled eyes turned shrewdly on Stewart during his cross-examination seemed to affect him strangely. His cross-examination lasted the whole of one afternoon, and there were one or two memorable moments in it.

"You know," said FitzAllen at one point, "that your finger-prints were on the knife, and that moreover they were the only finger-prints there?"

Stewart assented almost inaudibly.

"Can you explain that?"

"I suppose I must have used the knife some time during that day. I often play with it if I am sitting at my desk thinking."

"But that does not explain why there is only one set of finger-prints on it."

"No," said Stewart quietly without attempting to give any further explanation, and the counsel passed on to another question.

Later, when the question of the pre-selection gears came up, Stewart's answers were even less satisfactory. After he had told the Court about wishing to buy a new car as a reason for questioning the chauffeur, the counsel turned suddenly to him.

"And who did you intend to buy this car from?" he asked sharply.

There was a pause before Stewart replied, and a faint shadow seemed to cloud his eyes for a moment. "I had not actually taken the matter as far as that," he said at last. "I had heard much about the car and wanted to buy a new one, anyway, but I thought it best to find out a little about that particular sort of gear from Wilson before doing anything definite about it. I have a rather cautious nature," he went on with a slight smile, "and I always like to know the details of anything before I undertake it."

"And yet you asked your chauffeur the exact details of driving such a car? One would think the purchase very near for you to take such an interest in that side of the question. How often do you drive your own car, usually?"

"Very seldom," said Stewart, "but I think you over-estimate my interest. It was rather Wilson's mechanic's zeal. As far as I remember I merely asked him a general question as to their suitability, and the detailed answer I received was rather a reflection of his own interest than of mine."

When Freda entered the box the prosecuting counsel was frankly cynical. He asked her very few questions, merely revealing the fact that she had had no idea of the time she had seen the two figures in the drive. He appeared to attach little importance to the second figure. Moreover, the mechanic had not actually seen the other person but only what had seemed to be a movement in the bushes.

Slowly the case dragged on over a second and then into a third day. For the most time the court-room was intolerably hot and stuffy, and the terrible passiveness of the crowd seemed to be becoming intolerable to the prisoner. At the beginning of the case he had appeared not to notice them at all, but now whenever some sound, even of a cough, came from them, I could see his neck tighten suddenly and his hands clench together in his lap. He was showing the strain of these days very clearly, sometimes sitting for an hour or more staring at nothing without any movement or recognition that evidence was still being given and witnesses questioned.

Strangely enough, it was Mrs. Duncan's evidence which was the most damning in a way, for although she had very little to tell she stressed her late husband's devotion to the family so much that when she had finished it appeared that Duncan could only have committed suicide for one reason—to shield Stewart. Of course, she herself knew nothing, but I felt that her insistence on such phrases as "he knew a lot that he wouldn't tell," and "the knowledge was too much for him," could have only one interpretation placed on it by the jury.

The case for the prosecution, on the other hand, was brisk and to the point. One could see the hand of Stute behind it as each point was given and corroborated by finger-print experts, doctors, policemen, and Stute himself. Beef moved restlessly in his seat, but he appeared to be taking more interest in the case than he had been at first.

"Can't you think of anything at all?" I asked despairingly, but he simply shrugged his shoulders heavily.

"What can I do?" he said. "They won't use all the evidence I gave them now. I'd like to see what that Fitz, whatever his name is, would say to me if I told him there was poison in the whisky. I can't understand Sir William at all, he doesn't seem to have established the possibility of it being someone outside the house."

But the biggest surprise of the prosecution came when the last of their witnesses seemed to have been called and then we heard the name Wilkinson and remembered the "surly Tapster." I looked at Beef in astonishment. Neither of us had any idea that Stute had got on to the man, and since Beef had obtained nothing from him, we had rather easily assumed that he had nothing to tell.

He came into the court-room and entered the box with a deep scowl on his face as though the whole business was a criminal waste of his time. The counsel had some difficulty in extracting any information from him at all, but in little growls and short grudging sentences his evidence was pieced together. In effect it was that he had been the witness of a quarrel between Stewart and Dr. Benson. It had taken place some months back when he was still actively supervising the garden at the Cypresses. He was, he said, working in a part of the kitchen garden which was screened from the house by the row of cob-nut trees. Stewart and Benson had come out of the house in the middle of an argument and continued it on the lawn, so that he could hear the angry sound of their voices but could not gather what was the subject of their quarrel. Mr. Wilkinson was quite sure on this point. He did not know what the argument had been about—all he could say was that they had certainly argued. More than that, it had eventually become an almost uncontrolled fight with both men apparently threatening each other. At the height of it Dr. Benson had suddenly turned away and gone round the side of the house and Stewart had stamped indoors slamming the door behind him.

With this witness the prosecution completed their case. Watching the whole thing through, I was impressed by the widely different characters of the two lawyers and the methods they used to try to convince the jury of their case. It was not that either of them used anything else than the facts already produced in the court-room, but in their methods of seeing those facts one recognized something of the two men. Sir William Petterie spoke brilliantly, so that one felt behind his defence a great knowledge of men, a culture and an understanding that would perhaps, had he been a writer, have made of him one of the great humanitarians of which Zola is the best example. He did not try to trick his audience into believing something which he himself did not feel to be completely true, he tried to show in clear, forceful, and persuasive language the real human side of the case which the police's evidence ignored.

On the other hand, FitzAllen was cold and efficient, giving no more or less than the full value of each piece of evidence. He seemed to be saying to jury, "I'm only here to extract this for you—it is for you to decide its meaning and its importance." He had a straightforward case to present, the importance of which lay in the clear sequence of facts and evidence bearing on them. I thought he made his case in the shrewdest possible way. He too had much experience of mankind—but it was at the jury that he directed this knowledge. He seemed to have summed them up both as a group and as individuals.

At last came the judge's summing-up in cold concise terms, and then with slow and somewhat stiff dignity the jury rose to retire and consider their verdict.

Chapter XXVII

FROM the moments in which the jury filed slowly out of the Court I was convinced that there was no chance of an acquittal. Those twelve citizens, with two solid-looking women among them, would scarcely need to debate over the clear case which had been presented by the police. The brilliance of Sir William Petterie would in itself be suspect in their determination not to be hoodwinked by an obviously clever man, and a man of great culture and eloquence. They would automatically react against his persuasions. Shrewd little FitzAllen, who had contented himself with succinctly summarizing his powerful case and making no emotional appeal whatever, was far more what they wanted. For one afternoon at least he had played John Blunt, and though in fact I felt him to be the more cunning of the two great lawyers, this role would be the more likely to succeed.

Perhaps that was a more than usually solemn conscientious-looking jury, the sort of conclave of grimly pudding-like business men and women that one sees in American films being indifferent to the tearful verbiage of the hero's lawyer. They marched slowly out without looking back at the shrunken figure of Stewart Ferrers who was being removed by his warders.

"Time for a cup of tea," said Beef, jerking his thumb unnecessarily towards the exit.

"I should scarcely have thought there would be," I said with attempted irony, meaning to make him feel how completely the decision had already gone against the man he was defending.

"Oh yes, there is. A lot like that will want to have a good old talk over it. Besides, they wouldn't like to come back too quick as though they hadn't taken the time to go into everything."

"All right," I said, and we left the Court to find a basement café not far away.

I do not think that at any time during the case I was more convinced than then of Stewart's guilt, and if I was convinced, how could the jury be otherwise? But Beef sank lethargically into a chair and did not speak while we were waiting for the tea to be brought to us.

"Beef," I said, trying to disturb this phlegmatic dullness, "are you certain he's not guilty?"

"Yes, I'm certain," said Beef.

"Then, good Heavens, man, why can't you do anything? Do you realize that that jury is going to send him to the gallows as sure as fate?"

"I shouldn't be surprised if they found him guilty," admitted Beef.

"Well, then..."

"It's no good," Beef assured me, "I've done all I can. I found out everything there was to find out, and that's all there is to it."

"But don't you realize what this means? I've

tried to make you see how awful it will be for both of us if they hang an innocent man. Peter chose you to get the evidence to defend his brother, and it's on your shoulders. If he's hanged because you weren't clever enough to get at the truth, you'll never forgive yourself."

"Can't help that," said Beef glumly.

"Besides, think of your reputation. It's absolutely unheard of for a novelist's detective to fail. It'll be the first time it's ever happened. You'll have made a fool of yourself and me."

"Can't help it," Beef said, pouring out the tea which had been brought for us. "Do you take sugar?"

At that point a new idea suddenly came to me. I can't think why I had never thought of it before, or if I had unconsciously done so, why it had never registered.

"Do you think," I burst out, "that Stewart may be shielding someone? After all, there were a lot of things he wouldn't speak the truth about. Surely when a case is as desperate as this, even if the truth reflected badly on his character, he wouldn't consider it. Perhaps he knows who did it and is deliberately sacrificing himself."

Beef grunted. "Do you think that Stewart is the sort of man who would sacrifice himself?"

"Frankly, I don't know what kind of a man Stewart is. He's mystified me from the beginning. I know that I ought to be able to give a complete and snappy psychological portrait of anyone who comes into your cases, but this man defeats me."

"Ah," said Beef, and took a giant bite from a Bath bun.

Just then some of the witnesses in the case appeared in the doorway. Ed Wilson and Rose had had the same thought as we had. Beef flourished a tea-spoon towards them to attract their attention. They came to our table at my invitation and sat down. They were more welcome than the antique-dealer's wife who followed them, and made straight for us.

"I was lucky to get a seat, wasn't I?" she said, "but then I deserved it. I more than half expected you'd have two seats sent to me like the Theatre Royal do when I show their card in my window. I mean, I have helped with the case, haven't I? Do you think he'll get off?"

"No," said Ed Wilson, lighting a cigarette from the stump of another.

"He must have done it," said the antique-dealer's wife. "I mean, it came out plain, didn't it? Finger-prints on the knife, and everything. I haven't read all the cases I have done for nothing, you know. Besides, you could see he was guilty."

In spite of all this Beef remained stolid and indifferent. None of the woman's gossip, or of the obvious concern of Ed and Rose, seemed able to disturb his calm.

Ed Wilson in particular evidently felt the genuine concern of a decent young man faced by an abnormal tragedy.

"You know," he said, "he was always a funny

fellow, and you never quite knew where you were with him. But I shouldn't like to think of his being hanged if he didn't do it. I didn't like the way things went with him. That little lawyer there was clever, wasn't he?"

"But how do you know he didn't do it?" burst in the antique-dealer's wife. "In my opinion he's as guilty as he can be. I mean, who else would have had any reason to, that's what I say."

Rose looked very near tears. The strain of giving evidence, and seeing the man for whom she worked stand in the dock, had evidently told on her. "I think you're all horrible," she said, "the way you treat it as a peep-show. Even if he did do it, it's nothing to come and stare at. And Sergeant Beef said he didn't do it, and he ought to know."

Even that piece of flattery failed to rouse Beef to words.

"Ought to know, I daresay," went on the more garrulous woman. "But if he knows so much, why can't he find out who did do it? That's supposed to be a detective's job."

Ed Wilson made a gesture to silence her, for at that moment Peter and Sheila Benson came into the café together. They saw us and took a distant table, but I felt it my duty to go across and try to give them some encouragement. They asked me to sit down, and for the first time I was aware that on Peter Ferrers also the strain had told. He looked as though he had had a number of sleepless nights, and Sheila Benson was uncharacteristically quiet and unhappy. She only made one remark. "What a dreadful place a court is," she said feelingly, with a glance at Ferrers.

"I know," I said, "I've been sympathizing with you both all through the trial. But don't lose hope yet. One can't foresee the verdict."

"He will be found guilty," said Peter grimly.

And after a few minutes in which I tried to produce a few words of brightness and enlivenment, he looked at his watch and said that the jury had been out for an hour and that we had better get back.

As it transpired, he was perfectly right, for we hadn't been in our places more than ten minutes when the usher appeared.

Beef spoke at last. "Now for it," he whispered in my ear, and I realized that he was more deeply concerned than I had believed in the verdict which was to be given.

I knew that the correct thing for me to do was to study those jurymen's faces and try to discover in them some indication of what their verdict was to be. And I was relieved to find that they respected tradition sufficiently to show nothing. They sat comfortably in their places as though prepared for at least another hour of self-importance, and for a few minutes of real conspicuousness. They had been given, I reflected, for once in their lives, a chance to express themselves in a manner so profound and final that Dante or Shakespeare himself might have envied them. With one word they were to sway, not vaguely or remotely the emotions and hearts of an incalculably small number of their fellows, but the actual destiny of a man. Their clay, their paint, their notes, their words, were a human life.

The foreman, a little sparrow-like man with a few long hairs streaked obliquely over a dough-coloured head, rose when summoned and admitted in an almost falsetto voice that he and his fellow jurymen were agreed. He kept his eyes fixed on the judge while the next question was put to him, and in answer to it piped "Guilty" much more loudly than was necessary.

There was complete silence. Nobody fainted, nobody wept, nobody rose from his place. The prisoner glanced once towards the jury and then let his head sink forward. The whole mass of people in that court-room were either too appalled, or perhaps too pleased with their own prescience, to move or speak.

The judge cleared his throat to pronounce sentence, and we walked out into the open air after having heard that Stewart was to be hanged.

Chapter XXVIII

I DID not see Beef for some days after the trial, as I had left London. The verdict on that last day had shaken me so that although I knew that I should be unable to work, yet I had to get away from the case for a while. It was with something of a jolt that I realized how facile had been my philosophy during this and previous cases. Everything will come right in the end, I had seemed to say to myself, and however unsuccessful Beef's investigations might look at any particular moment, and however agitated I might be over his waste of time, I had felt all through that by some miraculous discovery Beef would be able to produce sufficient evidence on the day to exonerate Stewart and round off the book satisfactorily. But nothing of the sort had happened, and I saw for the first time how foolish it was to suppose that it could have done.

When, some three or four days later, a letter arrived from Beef, I opened it sceptically. Beef would not be likely to write unless there was some new "development," and I had lost faith in developments. I felt bitterly that the continued optimism of the Sergeant was now a very shabby cloak to hide his inefficiency.

The letter was written from his house in Lilac Crescent and dated the previous day.

DEAR T. (it said),

I had an interview yesterday with Sir William Petterie. I might say that he realizes better than some others I could mention the value of my work in this case,
and he has decided to appeal. I still feel that Justice may
win. I think you ought to have been here to have come to
that interview as it may turn out to be an important part
of the case.

Yours truly,
W. BEEF.

What case? I said to myself, studying his large
scrawl. There was no case. So far as I was concerned,
the past weeks had been a ghastly waste of time,
for quite obviously there was no story for me to
write. One couldn't write a detective novel in which
one's pet detective had believed the wrong man to
be innocent, and failed to find the guilty party.

. I had no hopes whatever of the appeal, and did
not take the trouble to find out on what grounds it
was based. Petterie's only hope, I felt, would be if
there had been some technical breach, or if the
judge could be thought to have summed up unfairly.
As Seebright's summary had been a dispassionate
and concise affair, and the trial had been con-
ducted with (as it seemed to me) exemplary for-
bearance, I could not build much hope on this. No, I
had to face it. Beef had failed, and I had failed with
him. I should have to look round now for some
other private investigator whose exploits would
furnish me with material for novels, and who
would not let me down in this humiliating way. I

regretted Beef because his personality enabled me to exercise that facetiousness which I believe is my forte, but I realized that I must cut my losses on him.

I had heard stories of an elderly clergyman in Worcestershire who had done some remarkable work, and seemed to have a personality fitted to this kind of fiction. He apparently never left his booklined study, but, puffing gently at his meer-schaum pipe, elucidated problems which were baffling the police of two continents. Perhaps, I thought, I could constitute myself his Boswell, if someone had not already found him. Belonging to a highly specialized profession—that of a private investigator's private crime writer—I realized that I might have some difficulty in finding another situation for myself. But it was obviously quite useless to continue with Beef. Stewart would be hanged, and when his corpse was shuffled underground, with it would be buried the last shreds of Sergeant Beef's reputation.

However, in the meantime I needed rest. I gave no thought to all the queer and rather sordid people we had met in Sydenham, did not allow myself to wonder whether Mrs. Duncan had purchased her public-house, or whether the antique-dealer's wife had found other suspicious characters to follow, dismissed from my nostrils the stench of old Fryer's yard, and the musty odour of the Cypresses, gave no thought to the two ill-assorted pairs of lovers: Ed Wilson and his quiet pale wife, and Peter

Ferrers with the doctor's talkative widow; did not ask if Freda had found herself another situation in which to exercise her talents for invective and breaking dishes; forgot the sinister face of Wakefield, and the narrow eyes and tight lips of Wilkinson, reverted no more to the young mechanic as a suspect, or the shadowy personality of Oppenstein, dismissed from my mind all those things which had once seemed clues; swordstick and key, bloodstain and paper stolen from Peter's room; turned, in other words, from all the mass of misery and ugliness which had made up the Sydenham murder case, and settled myself into the Norfolk countryside.

I used to get up at dawn and look for mushrooms, finding in that simpler search more satisfaction than I had known in the pursuit of evidence.

When the morning papers eventually gave news of the appeal, it seemed unreal to me, and by the time I came to read that the appeal had failed I was reconciled to the conviction that Stewart was guilty, and that he would be hanged. I was sorry for Beef, but like him I could do no more.

One morning, as I returned to the cottage in which I was staying, my landlady met me at the door and handed me a telegram.

"I hope there's no bad news," she said, coming from a class to whom telegrams are still fateful and sinister things. I read it with irritation.

MUST WRITE HOME SECRETARY URGENTLY NEED YOUR HELP PLEASE RETURN TO LONDON BEEF.

I turned this over in my hand for five minutes, until I was told that lunch was ready, and while I ate some excellent cold roast chicken I debated sourly over it. Why should I give up the peace and pleasure of this quiet and level countryside to return to London with no better object than to help Beef compose a letter which would in any case do no good now? There was nothing more for me to get from this case, and I only wanted to finish my holiday and start work afresh in new surroundings. I decided that I would not be called back to London in so forlorn a matter, and wired back that afternoon:

USELESS TO WRITE HOME SECRETARY CANNOT LEAVE MUCH NEEDED HOLIDAY ADVISE YOU ABANDON DETECTION AND PURCHASE PUBLIC HOUSE TOWNSEND.

Just before tea-time the postman, with an aggrieved look as though he took it as unfair that he should have to journey twice in one day to my cottage, handed me another telegram which I read with a sigh.

PREFER CUSTOMER'S SIDE OF COUNTER ARRIVE 8:10 BEEF.

Well, if he was nothing else, the Sergeant was tenacious. It seemed that he was not going to admit having blundered in this case until Stewart was actually hanged.

I felt perhaps slightly flattered at his mountain to Mohammed tactics, but at the same time realized again how little experienced in life he must be. First to think that a letter from him to the Home Secretary could help Stewart, and second, to need me to write it for him. However, I went down to the station to meet him.

He looked fitter and more cheerful, I thought, than when I had seen him during the trial, and it was the old Beef who, as he gripped my hand, asked what the darts were like at the local.

"I thought you'd come to get a letter written," I pointed out severely.

"Plenty of time for that tomorrow," said Beef. "He's not being hanged for a week, and I couldn't give my mind to anything of that sort after being shut up in a train all these hours. You and I will see the two best in the house. I hope you play better than you did in London. If you'd only keep them on the board it would be something."

That was all I could get out of him before we sat under the low beams of the *Anglian Maid*, and the rest of that evening was spent as Beef wished. I must own that he became very popular with the local customers whom he flattered by saying that they threw as pretty a dart as he had seen outside London.

But no sooner had we had breakfast next morning than he asked for pen and paper, and sat facing me across the little table.

"Now," he said, "you write, and I'll tell you what to say."

Out of charity, I suppose, out of sheer kind-heartedness for old Beef in these moments of his failure, I wrote the letter he asked, realizing that with every word that went down on paper how useless it would be. His clumsy flattery was my only reward.

"You don't half know how to put words together," he said before he thrust out a great length of tongue to lick the envelope. "He'll have to take some notice of that, won't he?"

And because I felt too dispirited by his optimism to argue, I said, "I suppose so," and left Beef to post our joint effort.

Chapter XXIX

BUT when the day for the execution of Stewart Ferrers approached I found that I could not remain placidly in the country. I grew nervous and irritable, and the kindly little Norfolk woman who was my landlady asked me more than once if I "wasn't well." It began to seem to me that I myself had been responsible for this approaching hanging of an innocent man. If, I argued miserably as I lay awake at night, a more competent detective than Beef had been called in, surely he would have found the evidence that would have cleared Stewart. Beef had discovered just enough to be sure that he had not done it, and not enough to be able to prove it. And then, I thought, the calling in of Beef had been my fault. For if I had not taken him up while he was still a village policeman and turned his lucky solutions into complicated triumphs, he would never have had enough reputation for Peter Ferrers to have employed him.

So, I said to myself, I was in part to blame, and there seemed to be nothing in the world I could do about it. If Stewart Ferrers had been a woman, or an imbecile, or if circumstances could have been produced which would have made the murder of

Benson in any way forgivable, there might have been a chance of persuading the Home Secretary to listen to a public appeal signed by a great number of influential people. But the murder had been a brutal one, and the actions of Stewart, as presented by the police, merited as severe a punishment as that given to any murderer. There seemed to be no hope.

After fighting for some days against the inclination to return to London, I suddenly decided to pack my bags and go back. It was not that I felt I could do anything, but at least I wanted to be on the spot and not showing so much indifference to the hideous fate of the man who was to be hanged. I found Beef himself in a somewhat agitated state, though not as profoundly stirred as one would have expected.

"Where it comes in," he said, "is when you've had years and years of dealing with all sorts of things. You get blunted. I remember a young fellow sent to prison for a month over a house-breaking job. And it turned out he'd only been frightened into doing what he had done by a whole gang of men what we arrested nicely afterwards. And there was another case of a lady suspected of robbing a mission box who..."

"Don't let's go into your past achievements as a policeman," I said sharply. "This is much too serious."

"I know it's serious," Beef returned. "I'm only saying that I'm accustomed to having tragedy through my hands."

"What has been done since I was here?" I asked.

"Well, I sent my letter off to the Home Secretary telling him all the reasons I had for thinking it wasn't Stewart. I only had a printed slip in reply saying that it had been received."

"Did you expect anything more?" I asked.

"Well, it was a long letter, wasn't it?" Beef pointed out.

"So that the poor chap's going to be hanged on Thursday?"

"That's right. Horrible business too."

"And you don't think it's your fault?"

" 'Course it isn't," said Beef. "You don't blame a doctor when he works to save a patient and can't, do you? I've done my best, as I've told you before."

I got up hurriedly, feeling that I could not stand any more of Beef's complacent murmurings. Beef followed me into the hall, and just at that moment the telephone bell rang.

"Here, wait a minute," said Beef, picking up the receiver, "it might be something."

"I don't doubt it," I said coldly; "at least a wrong number," and I went on towards the door. But something in Beef's voice as he answered the 'phone stopped me with my hand on the knob.

"But what is it?" he kept insisting, and then after a few moments of puzzled listening, "Hallo? Hallo?" He put the instrument down and looked at me almost guiltily.

"It's something new come up," he said. "That was that antique-dealer's wife. She said it was important, but she wouldn't tell me what it was. Said we was to come down."

This time I made no protest as the two of us got into the car. By now the journey had become something of a penance, and I knew that Beef understood my protest without my taking the trouble to make it. But what, I thought viciously to myself, could that interfering old woman have discovered now that would be worth driving across London for. That Fryer was not the old tramp's real name, or some such useless piece of inquisitiveness, I supposed. Now that Beef had started her off on the idea that anyone could be a detective, she looked like being something of a menace.

Beef was silent as we drove along, and I had time to attempt to clarify my thoughts about the whole case. While I had been away in Norfolk the danger in which Stewart stood of being hanged had tortured me. But now that I had returned to London the whole atmosphere seemed to have changed. Somehow it was inconceivable that this thing could come about. I had accepted the fact that a crime-writer's detective could actually fail to discover the guilty person in a case, or, as in the present one, be incapable of saving an innocent man's life. But was it really possible? It was a thing that had never been allowed to happen before, and with that huge and influential precedent behind it, could it happen now? Since the case had started in such a stereotyped way, was it possible that it would finish with a last-minute rescue?

This seemed the only possible ending. We had begun the whole thing under the worst possible conditions. Perhaps Beef was really to blame, not for being inefficient, but for being so naïve as to set up near Baker Street. I began to feel that, even more important than saving Stewart from the gallows, I must rescue the case from the hackneyed ending of a last-minute rescue. Perhaps in this very drive down to Sydenham I was helping to bring to light just the one piece of evidence that Beef needed.

But I need not have worried myself about this, for the first words the antique-dealer's wife spoke when we drew up once more in front of the shop were exciting enough even if they were half expected.

"She's run away," she said even before the car had stopped moving. "I don't know what it means, but it seems very queer to me. I said to myself, there's one man who ought to know about this straight away, and that's Sergeant Beef, I said. He may not have been able to find enough to get Mr. Ferrers off, I said, but perhaps this is just the evidence he's been waiting for."

Beef spoke without moving from the car. "And what have you found out?" he said. "Who's run away?"

"Why, Mrs. Benson," said the woman with surprise. "Left without telling nobody. Sold all her furniture to my cousin who's got a second-hand business near the Crystal Palace, and took the first price he offered without arguing. 'It's not natural,' he said to me, and I could see it had given him quite a shock, and him with his bad heart. Anyway, there it is, and if you go up to Doctor Benson's house you can see that I'm not telling you a lie."

And indeed it was quite obvious that the woman had not invented the story even from the gateway of the house.

"But, Beef," I protested as he began to get out of the car as if he were going to make sure that the house was indeed empty, "what does it matter if she has gone? You couldn't expect her to live in that house by herself. The obvious thing for her to do was to move. I expect she's moved into a furnished flat in town somewhere. I don't see that this has the slightest importance."

"Well, you can't tell," said Beef cautiously. "But why that silly woman couldn't tell me over the 'phone. . ."

It was with something of a sense of flatness that I dropped Beef at his house in Lilac Crescent. There was a feeling of incompleteness about this stage of the affair which I could not pin down to any special causes. I merely felt that something should be done on this last day. Surely, I thought, Beef should be seeing people, searching, at least doing something instead of going home like a comfortable shopkeeper at the end of his day. Tomorrow, unless he could prevent it, Stewart would be hanged. Even if I could achieve nothing useful I felt impelled to see some of the people involved and find out if anything was being done. With this feeling for activity for its own sake I drove round to the block of flats in which Peter lived.

The porter on duty was the same man that Beef had interviewed, and I told him that I wanted to see Peter Ferrers.

"Mr. Ferrers is not in," he said shortly.

"What time will he be back?"

"He won't be in to anyone," the man said, eyeing me with some hostility.

Thinking perhaps that Peter felt that he should be left to face his tragedy alone, I left without further protest, only asking the porter to tell Mr. Ferrers that I had called.

What else could I do? Where else could I go? While I was quite willing to admit that this last-minute rushing round London was useless, I felt, too, that it was inevitable. No one could stay still and passively wait. But there was one man who, I felt, would give me a more satisfactory interview, and that was Brian Wakefield. I had not called on him at his flat before, but I remembered his address in Blackfriars from a conversation between Beef and Peter Ferrers. Now I drove over, and after a little difficulty in locating it—Peter had said it looked like a block of offices—knocked on the door.

Wakefield seemed quite pleased to see me and invited me in. Quite cynically, I think, he had made a quick analysis of my state, and the rôle of psycho-analyst pleased him. But I was too worried to resent his rather friendly, superior tone when he said:

"Well, what's on your mind?"

Yet in a way this interview was as hopeless as the other. I myself could scarcely explain the unrest which I felt, and although Wakefield must have sensed it, there was nothing he could do.

"What do you think about this case now?" I asked him at last. "Now all the evidence has been sifted and the trial over, what do you think about the verdict?"

Wakefield sucked slowly at his pipe and seemed to be considering the question, although in reality he was wondering how far he could be frank with me.

"Well, to be perfectly honest," he said slowly, "I think Stewart did it. Of course, you'll remember my saying some time ago that I thought he was capable of commiting a murder. The police's case seemed pretty water-tight to me."

More than his words, it was his attitude which affected me. He might have been sitting back watching a minor chemical experiment taking place. In any case, I could see that the hanging of Stewart Ferrers, whether innocent or guilty, meant very little to him.

"Let's see," he went on, "the hanging is tomorrow morning, isn't it? That is something which has always interested me—the psychological state of man during those few last hours before he is hanged. You have, of course, read that superb passage of Dostoevsky's in *The Idiot* where the Prince describes his feelings under similar circumstances?"

But my mind was preoccupied with the more immediate thought of the present condemned man.

"What does Peter think?" I asked.

"I have not, of course, told him what I think," said Wakefield. "He himself seems to hold out some hope of a last-minute reprieve. Really, I hadn't the heart to disillusion him."

There was clearly no peace of mind to be gained here, but somehow I had not the energy to move. Wakefield talked amazingly well, and his voice was like a drug to me in my present condition. It took my mind completely away from what had been its foremost consideration during the greater part of the last few weeks, and when at last I left some time after midnight I felt that at least I should sleep soundly. I had arranged to meet Beef fairly early to take him round to the prison.

Long before nine o'clock on that fatal morning Beef and I walked along in a light drift of rain near Pentonville prison. The street about us was reasonably busy, but it was a gloomy street for all that, with greyish Victorian buildings the stucco of which was decaying.

Beef scarcely spoke until we reached a young policeman on point-duty.

"Where do they show the black flag?" he asked abruptly.

"Eh?" said the policeman.

Beef coughed. "I'm ex-Sergeant Beef," he explained. "I've been concerned in the Ferrers case, and I've got to see the last of it. D'you mind telling me where the black flag goes up?"

"You'll see it round the other side," said the

policeman rather grumpily, disapproving perhaps of anything so morbid.

In a wider but a less busy street we found a group of bedraggled people who had evidently come here with the same object as Beef and I. None of them were familiar to us, and I was relieved, though perhaps a little puzzled, by the absence of Peter Ferrers. These people seemed somehow dispirited and bottlenecked, and I wondered that their curiosity should be strong enough to keep them standing in the rain for the gloomy satisfaction of knowing that a man had been hanged.

"Do you think," I asked Beef, "that there may be still a chance? Wakefield told me last night that Peter still had hopes. It wouldn't be an unheard-of thing if the Governor had received last-minute instructions, would it?"

Beef made no answer except for a sudden grip of my arm and an indication to where, high on that dismal building, a small square of black had suddenly started to flutter against the grey sky.

"Stewart's hanged," he said, and then as he turned away, "And I suppose I'm ruined."

Chapter XXX

Even then, Beef's reputation, or what there was of it, might have been saved if it had not been for his inordinate vanity. Within forty-eight hours of the curt paragraphs which appeared in the daily press to announce that Stewart Ferrers, the Sydenham murderer, had been hanged that morning, Angus Braithwaite, the star crime reporter of one of our most popular dailies, heard, it appears, of Beef's part in the investigations. The case had not been an exciting one from the journalistic point of view, and Braithwaite was not satisfied with the many and varied intimate sidelights he had thrown on it. His interview with Sheila Benson had not been as revealing as one might have supposed, and his story about Ed Wilson and Rose, "building life anew on the shambles of this ugly case," though in the tradition of his paper, had not satisfied him.

So Braithwaite at least blessed Beef. Like everyone else who reads crime novels as well as studying crime, Braithwaite had frequently been irritated by the ease and assurance with which private investigators strolled through the maze of evidence, calmly taking the one preordained path towards veracity. He had felt, as he had observed the masters in action, from Holmes and Blake to

Thorndike and Mason, peeved by their certainty of success. And now at last, he realized, a private investigator had failed. With immense delight he sharpened his reporter's pencil, jumped into a taxi, and made for Lilac Crescent.

And Beef, of course, fell right into it. As he told me afterwards, he was accustomed to giving the details to the reporters on the local papers in the various places in which he had been stationed as a policeman, and this more impressive journalist did not disturb him.

"Sergeant Beef?" Braithwaite asked with a smile, and, like Snow White receiving the Witch, Beef accepted the apple of his cordiality and asked him in.

"I'm from the *Daily Dose*," said Braithwaite, "and we're very interested in your work in connection with this Sydenham case."

"Oh yes?" said Beef, delighted, I imagine, by this attention.

"We have heard," Braithwaite went on, "that you collected some remarkable evidence which was never produced in Court."

"I wouldn't say that," said Beef. "I think Sir William Petterie used everything I gave him that could be any help. The trouble was I couldn't say who had done it."

I can imagine Braithwaite's difficulty in suppressing his pleasure at those artless words. He sat there talking to the Sergeant for the best part of an hour, and without much difficulty got the whole story. How he had been successful in two previous murder mysteries, how he had set up on his own, how Peter Ferrers had come to him as being, he told Braithwaite, the man most obviously possessed of brilliance, insight, intuition, psychology, and all the other qualities which the Sergeant most envied in his rivals, how he had undertaken the case and set about the investigations. He went on to explain in detail his conviction that Stewart was innocent, and the odds and ends of evidence he had unearthed and which the police had ignored. Without realizing apparently the harm he was doing himself, he enlarged on his disappointment at failing to discover the real murderer, his chagrin at not being called as a witness, his sense of responsibility for the hanging of Stewart Ferrers when, as he still maintained, "Stewart had no more murdered Doctor Benson than he, Beef, had." He described our visit to Pentonville and our sense of dismay when the black flag had eventually appeared. And he showed Braithwaite out, unconscious, I am convinced, that this criminologist as he called himself took with him a story that would flutter the dove-cotes of crime fiction, and bring the Sergeant into hopeless and irrevocable discredit.

It was not until next morning when he went out to purchase the *Daily Dose* in the vain and complacent belief that he would see no more than a photograph of himself with a caption explaining that he had done good work in the Sydenham murder case that Beef was aware of the truth. The photograph was there, the caption was different.

PRIVATE INVESTIGATOR FAILS

VILLAGE SHERLOCK HOLMES COULD NOT SAVE MAN FROM
GALLOWS

*Sergeant Beef, Amateur Detective Hero of Two Novels,
Makes History by Defeat*

I sat today in the small front room of a house near Baker Street and talked to a man with a broken heart. Since Sherlock Holmes chose it Baker Street has been considered the Harley Street of detection, and when some months ago ex-Sergeant William Beef decided to set up as a private investigator, he selected this district. Full of hope and confidence, he displayed his name-plate. He had solved two murder mysteries, and his biographer, Lionel Townsend, believed that he could solve others.

Today he is a fallen star. For the first time in the history of crime or crime fiction, the private investigator, the superhuman detective, the Holmes, the Sexton Blake, has failed to solve a mystery.

For Sergeant Beef, hero of *Case for Three Detectives*, and *Case Without a Corpse*, believed that Stewart Ferrers, the Sydenham murderer, was innocent. He was employed by Ferrers's brother to prove this and to find the guilty person.

Beef still believes him innocent, but he was unable to prove it and yesterday Ferrers was hanged.

There was gloom over the little house as I sat there drinking tea. "I never thought it would come to this," said Sergeant Beef, and buried his face in his hands. Mrs. Beef, staunch comrade of the Sergeant through all his vicissitudes, who had helped him in many of his cases, said that she felt this was the end. "I can hardly believe it," she told me as she wiped a tear away. "William's father was a policeman, and my father was employed to serve summonses by the Bromley County Court. Nothing like this has ever happened to us before."

When I tried to console Beef he shook his head. "It's all over," he whispered. "I couldn't find the murderer. They tell me this is the first time a book detective has failed. I am sorry because the disgrace has hurt my wife." He stretched out his arm, and the strong hand of the detective which had fallen on so many criminals' shoulders shook a little as it gripped his wife's, toil-worn and trembling. "We shall go away and start anew," said Mrs. Beef. I left them, with bowed heads, wondering what the future held for them.

I did not buy the *Daily Dose* until ten o'clock that morning when someone had pointed out to me what it contained. But when I saw the cutting I hurried round to Lilac Crescent. I had expected to find Beef angry, but I had never seen him in quite such a condition of taurine rage.

"I'll knock his blasted block off," were the words he greeted me with. "Hand shook a little! What's he take me for, a jellyfish?"

"Well, it's your own fault, Beef," I said, reasonably enough. "You shouldn't have answered his questions."

"How was I to know he was a snake in the grass?" asked Beef truculently. "He came here and complimented me on what I'd done in the case."

"Oh, Beef, Beef," I said sadly, "will you never learn anything about human nature? All he wanted was a story for his paper, and, good gracious, haven't you given him one!"

"Yes, and I'll give him another," said Beef, rising to his feet, "and one he can't print, or not in his paper, anyway. There's many a time when I was in the Force I'd like to have had a go at one of these chaps, and couldn't because of my uniform. But there's nothing to stop me now. Talk about tears in Mrs. Beef's eyes! *His* mother won't know who he is when he comes home tonight."

"Don't be ridiculous, Beef. You'd never be able to see him even if you did go down to the offices of the *Daily Dose*."

Beef hesitated. "No," he said, "I suppose they'd know what I was after. But I'll catch him one day, you see if I don't. Hiding my face in my hands! He'll have to hide his face in his hands when I've done with it."

"You're not the only sufferer from that sort of thing," I pointed out. "People are reported as behaving in that manner every morning."

"So they may be, but perhaps they can't all take care of themselves."

"You might realize," I said, "how I look. You don't think it's very pleasant for me, do you? It's not only yourself you've ruined by failing in this case, and giving that interview, but me too. Here I've been working to build up a reputation for you, and the whole thing's smashed. If you did ever get another case there's not a publisher in London would use the story of it."

How right I was in those words was shown next morning when the *Daily Dose* returned to the attack.

DETECTIVE'S FAILURE STARTLES WRITERS
Investigators Disturbed by Unheard-of Collapse

Writers of detective novels met in gloomy silence in their clubs yesterday following Angus Braithwaite's exposure of a failure by one of their creations. They are asking themselves where this will lead.

Since Sergeant Beef, Townsend's "master mind" of detection, admitted that he had believed Stewart Ferrers innocent and could not prove it, they feel that the future is insecure.

"Suppose this sort of thing becomes common," said one of them to a Daily Dose *reporter yesterday. "What will happen to crime novels? The public will lose confidence in our investigators and our circulation will fall by many thousands."*

"It is most unfortunate," said a well-known publisher of crime novels, "and a very dangerous precedent. If novelists' investigators cannot solve the problems created, who in the world can?"

Lord Simon Plimsol, distinguished amateur detective and hero of many ingenious cases, gave another view when we saw him in his West End flat yesterday. "Borin' business to find on return from one's honeymoon," he sighed, "though I've always anticipated that someone would get themselves into a mess some day."

In answer to a long-distance telephone call to the Near East, Monsieur Amer Picon, who has so brilliantly solved many more intricate cases than this, cabled enigmatically *"Hélas!* Mon Dieu. Je ne sais quoi," were his words to the *Daily Dose.*

Monsignor Smith waved his sunshade despairingly. "If the investigator fails to arrest the criminal," he said, "it can only be a matter of time before the criminal succeeds in arresting the investigator. If the novelist cannot find the end of the case, the case must be the end of the novelist."

I sank back into my armchair when I read this half-column of staring type. I realized that, for Beef and me, our brief attempt to invade this realm was finally frustrated.

Chapter XXXI

A NUMBER of weeks passed in which I heard no more of the Sydenham murder case, and I thought about it as little as possible. No one likes to be humiliated, and my own feelings were bitter.

Besides, I was looking to the future, and realized that I had to find another subject for my Boswellian efforts. I went down to Worcester to interview the parson of whom I had heard, but found another novelist already entrenched in the vicarage and busily following the Reverend Duncan Hardacre through the intricacies of a local poisoning. Neither of them welcomed me in the least, and the novelist was inclined to be rude when I explained what had brought me down.

I was becoming extremely anxious about the future, in fact, when to my surprise I received a telephone call from Beef.

"The time has come," he said, "at which I can give you further details."

I resigned myself to one last visit to Lilac Crescent, and drove round there the next day.

"Sit down," said Beef unexpectedly, "and I'll tell you all."

"All?" I repeated.

"All," he said.

"Do you mean to say that at this point you've suddenly discovered the truth about that business?"

"Never mind at what point I discovered it. You're going to hear it now. Sit still and I'll tell you the real facts about the Sydenham murders."

"Murders?" I gasped, genuinely surprised. "Do you mean to say there were two murders?"

"Three," said Beef calmly, and lit his pipe.

"Are you serious?"

"Absolutely serious," said Beef.

At this point I saw the futility of further interruptions. Beef would have to tell the story in his own way and I would have to sit and listen to it.

"All right, go ahead," I conceded, and he began.

"The trouble with you, T.," he said with irritating condescension, "is that you don't notice things. If you'd noticed things all through this case you wouldn't need to come to me now to hear what I know. For instance, the very first thing that happened was Peter coming here, wasn't it?"

"Yes," I said, "I noticed that."

"Ah, but what did I say to him?" asked Beef.

"So far as I remember, there was some harking back to one of your ridiculous darts championships."

"Ex-actly," said Beef, "ex-actly. Now, if instead of calling that ridiculous you'd have taken some notice of it, it would have led you to the truth. You see that was an important darts championship, for a silver cup presented by old Mr. Ferrers."

"Well?" I said.

"Doesn't that show," asked Beef, "that he was a gentleman? A gentleman," he repeated impressively, "in every sense of the word. I met him at the time. One of the best you ever met. No narrow-mindedness about him, I can tell you. He offered that cup, and he presented it himself, and George Watson and me won it."

"George Watson and *I*," I corrected quietly.

"You!" roared Beef—"you can't get a dart on the board."

"I was correcting your grammar," I explained icily, and Beef went on.

"At any rate, as you'll see later," he said, "my knowing and respecting that old gentleman has made all the difference. But now I'll tell you the story. Only, mind you,"—he stretched a blunt forefinger towards me—"it *is* only a story, and I couldn't prove it in a court of Law. At least, not without finding more evidence, and I'm not going to start that now. But you shall have it as I see it, right from the start.

"When it was clear that Benson was blackmailing Stewart, did it never occur to you to wonder what he was blackmailing him with? You can't get several sums of five hundred pounds out of a man without you know something pretty serious about him. Well, I can tell you what it was. He was blackmailing him with the murder of his own father."

"But old Ferrers died two years ago. There was nothing irregular about his death. Not even an inquest. There was a death certificate. . ."

"Yes, and who signed it?" asked Beef triumphantly. "The two of them were in it together. Stewart was in debt. More than that, he was in the hands of moneylenders. He was in a desperate position. He knew his father's money would come to him when the old gentleman died, but he needed it at once, so he decided to murder him. And he went about it in a way more criminals would have used if there were more doctors like Benson about. He made a pact with Benson. 'If I poison the old man,' he said, 'will you sign the death certificate and make everything regular? And I'll pay you so much.' Benson agreed and supplied him with the poison."

"Where's your proof of all this?" I asked.

Beef held up his hand. "Steady, steady," he said. "All in good time. As I was saying, Benson supplied the poison with instructions to Stewart as to how to give it him. Stewart gave it him, the poor old gentleman croaked, and there was Benson, the trusted family doctor, to make everything smooth and right. But the two of them overlooked one thing—that was young Peter. He was fond of his father, and wouldn't never have got mixed up in anything of that sort. If you remember, the butler told us (though I daresay you didn't take any notice of it at the time) that he was with his father right up to the end, *and afterwards*. It's my belief he was there when Benson came to examine old Mr. Ferrers, and saw the doctor remove the rest of the medicine into which Stewart had put the poison."

"What makes you think that?"

"Well, Benson wasn't going to leave it there, was he, if he knew what was in it? 'Course he wasn't. He took it away and took it back to his surgery. But he didn't destroy it. Perhaps he had some idea of blackmailing Stewart with it, or he may just have forgotten to destroy it, but anyway, there it was in his dispensary."

"How long?" I asked.

"Till Peter broke into the house and took it. That's another thing you didn't take any notice of, isn't it?—Sheila Benson saying there was a burglary there. It interested me, a burglary did. I know a bit about burglaries. I haven't been a sergeant for nothing. 'Why,' I said to myself, 'should anyone want to burgle a house like Benson's? Specially when he never went farther than the surgery according to Sheila Benson's account, and never took anything of any value. No, that aroused my suspicions."

"All this," I pointed out, "is the merest supposition."

"Do give me a chance to make my case," pleaded Beef with pretended exasperation. "When Peter got that medicine by breaking into Benson's dispensary he decided to make sure that what he thought was right. So he sent it off to an analyst, and the analyst gave him a report showing the medicine was chockfull of poison."

"How do you know that?" I asked again.

"I'll tell you," said Beef. "Did you hear me ask Peter for the address of an analyst? Did you never think to yourself that I could have found out on my own who was the best analyst to send anything to? Do you think I should ask anyone mixed up in the case for an analyst's address without having some reason for it? Well, I did have some reason. I was just hoping he would give me an analyst that he knew himself; that he'd used before. The one, in fact, to whom he'd sent the poison that murdered his father.

"And he did. The man not only analysed the whisky I took him, but he told me all I wanted to know about his last job for Peter. This bottle of medicine was sent in, quite ordinary medicine, containing so much of such and such a poison, and the analyst had made that report to Peter.

"But Peter had something else, something which proved to him that the two of them had worked together. How he'd got it I don't know, and I don't suppose we ever shall know. But he had, securely tucked away, the very piece of paper on which Benson had written his instructions when he gave the stuff to Stewart. 'Add this to the medicine,' he'd written, and sent whatever poison it was. So Peter knew what he was up to. He knew Benson was in it by supplying the poison and giving a death-from-natural-causes sort of certificate. He knew his brother was in it because he'd received those instructions from Benson, and hadn't never said afterwards anything about it, which he would have done had Benson been swinging it. I imagine that Peter actually noticed Benson packing up the bottle of medicine and taking it away with him, and perhaps that was what aroused his suspicions. Then he went through his brother's papers and found that little note in Benson's writing, and then he knew just where he was.

"But in the meantime the old gentleman's body had been cremated, and what was the good of a bit of paper and a bottle of medicine to bring home the crime to those two that were guilty? He saw for himself he wouldn't have a chance of getting them convicted, so he kept quiet and waited his time."

"Good Lord," I said, for I began to see it all.

"He wasn't half clever," reflected Beef, "and he didn't mean to take any chances. He was fond of his father and he meant to avenge the old man against those as had done the dirty on him. And he worked out a way in which he could do it neat and final. And he did too. That's how there were three murders. The murder of old Ferrers by Benson and Stewart, the murder of Benson, and the murder of Stewart by faking the evidence and getting him hanged. Three of them, and you thought there was only one." Beef almost chuckled.

"You never noticed another thing," Beef went on. "Old Ferrers was cremated. That was done in case there was any question as to how he died. But to make it reasonable, Benson's been recommending cremation ever since, and he's had dozens cremated. See how it all works out?"

Chapter XXXII

"P<small>ETER</small>'s idea," said Beef, "was to murder one of them himself in such a way as would get the other one hanged for doing it. What do you say to that? Clever, wasn't it? The first thing he had to do was to find a motive. He didn't know anything about the blackmailing or he wouldn't have needed to have looked any further. He had, in fact, to *make* a motive.

"We know how he did that. Wherever we turned in Sydenham we heard that story about Sheila Benson and Stewart. And wherever we tried to trace it to its origin, we failed. Why? Because it had no origin. I been studying American methods lately." Beef paused grandly. "Have you ever heard of a whispering campaign? They use it over there for almost anything—to ruin a politician, or to make a book popular. Well, Peter Ferrers started one all on his own to create a motive for a murder what hadn't yet been committed. He made everyone in Sydenham start talking about his brother and Sheila Benson, and as you know, people are always too ready to talk. You saw that parson jump up like a trout when we mentioned Stewart and Sheila Benson. I bet there wasn't one of his congregation who hadn't enjoyed it. And it would have been the same all round.

"Having got that going he was ready to think

279

out his actual method. He had plenty of time, and he didn't mean to make any mistakes. He fixed that day for it when he and Wakefield were going there to dinner with Benson in the house, at a time when only Stewart could have been there to do it. Benson had to be found stabbed by a knife on which Stewart's finger-prints were the only ones. So the first thing he does is to get hold of a book what hasn't got its pages cut, and which he could persuade Stewart to read out of that very evening.

"I remember you grinning at me silly when I was pretending to be pleased at having found out which part he'd read of that poem by seeing where he'd cut the pages. Actually I was pleased because I'd seen how he got Stewart's finger-prints on to that knife handle.

"Well, he brought the book down with Wakefield, but Wakefield didn't help matters by trying to get Stewart to back the paper. They went through to the library, and Peter suggested that his brother should read those favourite verses to them which Stewart, unsuspecting, did. Then Peter and Wakefield left the house and drove back to London.

"Peter left Wakefield at his lodgings, and put his car into the garage and told them that he wouldn't be wanting it again that night. Then he chatted to his porter at the block of flats, and went upstairs. That was all the alibi he needed. But what did he do? Went out by the service lift and walked round to the place where he'd got a hired car waiting."

"A hired car?" I repeated.

"Well, I'm only supposing that," admitted Beef, "but it would have been the easiest thing for him to do. He could have got a U-Drive a few days before and kept it handy. If we had to prove this whole thing, we could trace where he got it. Then he drove back to Sydenham and waited for Benson to come out of the Cypresses. Now if Benson had gone home at once, he'd have been sunk. He knew that, and was quite prepared to wait for another occasion, as he may have waited on previous occasions. But Benson didn't go home, and we know that Stewart showed him out at a quarter-past eleven, which would have given Peter plenty of time to get back to Sydenham from his flat. When he sees the lights in the library, he does what he's planned to do, walks over to the summer-house and gets that old swordstick what was lying about there. Then there he is in the drive waiting for Benson.

"Presently the front door opens. He hears Benson and Stewart say good night, and he's ready to speak to the doctor as he leaves. He tells him he has something important to talk over with him, as we know he had—his own affair with Sheila Benson. He's told her to prepare the doctor for this talk, so that Benson's already half expecting it. They take a few turns round the roads, and then on some pretext or other Peter leads him back to the house. Perhaps he suggested drawing up a memorandum of what they'd agreed, and signing it, or perhaps he said he would give him a cheque. At any rate, he got him back into the library. And when he was in the armchair, he outs with his swordstick and runs him through the neck before he could say knife."

"Knife?" I repeated.

"Yes, knife," said Beef. "That's what people do say, isn't it? But he was very careful. He's got his gloves on, and he wipes the swordstick off on the cushion and then picks up the Italian dagger with his brother's finger-prints on it, and digs it in the wound. Cold-blooded if you like, but you've got to remember the provocation. Then he notices the parcel that Benson has under his arm and sees it's treasury notes. He leaves these beside the corpse as though they were something to do with it and steps quietly out of the front door.

"Then he has a nasty shock. Just at that moment the young mechanic comes cycling in at the front gate, to report to Benson that he can't have his car that night. Peter hops back in the bushes and waits, leaving foot-prints that the police would have found next morning if they'd known their job, but which were washed away long before I got on the case. He sees the mechanic go up to the front door, and perhaps he hears him ring a couple of times, then, getting no answer, start cycling away. Peter realizes the danger of the mechanic's ringing having woken someone up in the house, someone who might find the corpse, so he's in a bit too much hurry to get away, and he bobs out of those bushes before the mechanic's out of the drive. The mechanic spots him, or thinks he spots some movements there and turns round and calls out 'Who's there?'"

so that Peter has to dodge back again. But the mechanic doesn't wait, and cycles away.

"Peter gets back to his car round the corner, and drives off back to London congratulating himself on having done a nice job of work. He leaves his hired car wherever he kept it and walks into his flats at two o'clock in the morning when there's no one on duty in the hall, and is lying comfortably asleep when they call him in the morning. Oh, but I forgot something," said Beef quickly; "before he left the Cypresses, he walked round again to the summer-house and put the swordstick back where he found it—not having touched it without his gloves on—and chucked his latch-key (which he had always had, though he deliberately hadn't used it) into the bushes."

"Why did he do that?" I asked.

"It was the best thing he could do," Beef explained. "If he was found with that latch-key on him it would be proof that he *could* have done the job, and if he'd thrown it away anywhere else and it had happened to be found it might have been tied up with him. Whereas a spare latch-key found near the house it belonged to could have been anyone's."

I nodded. "Go on," I said.

"But something had happened he couldn't have anticipated. Old Fryer, who used to get boozed and sleep anywhere handy, had stumbled in there in the evening and gone off to sleep. Whether he was there when Peter fetched the swordstick, or whether he was only there when he put it back, or whether he wasn't there at all until afterwards, I don't know. But he got there before the morning, and sobering up at daylight he looked round the summer-house to see if there was something he could knock off. He saw the swordstick, and being a cunning old beggar accustomed to dealing with all sorts of goods, he knew what it was and had an idea of the value of it. So he picks it up, and he's marching out of the gate with it when Ed Wilson comes in on his motor-bike.

"Well, you know what he did with it, and you know how we came to find it. And you remember your nasty sneers at the time because I happened to be interested in buying a dart-board. That dart-board led us to the truth!

"There's something in this case," Beef went on after a thoughtful pause, "that I think you'd call irony. That is that if Peter was to have kept out of it altogether the whole thing would probably have been done for him just as he wished. For why? Because Stewart himself had made up his mind to murder Benson, whose blackmailing had gone beyond all bounds. Now we know that Stewart was funny with money, we know that he'd been in the hands of moneylenders before his father died and had probably murdered his dad to get out of them. Also we know that he'd drawn out four sums of five hundred pounds each in single notes from his bank, and my guess would be that he'd agreed to pay Benson five hundred pounds a year for his part in that job, and that Benson wasn't satisfied with this. Benson had been agitating for an extra five hundred, and in case he'd have to pay it Stewart had drawn it out ready and kept it locked up in his bedroom. That evening he'd laid his little plans for doing Benson in. Suicide this was going to look like. He had a bottle of whisky handy into which he'd poured arsenic.

"Then he was going to make Benson sign what would look like a last note left by a suicide, drive him in his own car to some place, put the arsenic bottle in his hand and push him in the driving-seat, leaving him there with the confession on him. It was very simple, and might have worked out nicely. Only what happened? Well, you know what happened. Benson's car was under repair, so he came without it. Stewart saw that this wasn't the night to commit the murder, gave him the ordinary whisky and didn't use the bottle he'd prepared with the arsenic in it at all. But since Benson got nicely tiddled he didn't see why he shouldn't get the suicide note signed, seeing that it would come in handy for the next time. And Benson signed it like a bird as soon as he'd got his five hundred, mistaking it, as Stewart had meant him to, and as even the police saw he had, for a receipt. You see they'd been quarrelling, and the old question of what had happened to the poisoned medicine arose again, because that was Benson's lever on Stewart. Benson had to bluff on that because actually Peter had taken it. But he did bluff. 'It's in my surgery now,' he said, and Duncan heard it. But that was all before he'd got him tiddly, and before he'd signed the receipt.

"Then Stewart went off to bed cursing his luck that he'd had to pay out another five hundred and determined to wait for another occasion. He'd seen Benson off the premises, so he had nothing to worry about and was probably just as sound asleep as Duncan said he was when he took his tea up in the morning.

"When the hue and cry got going he never thought of that faked confession in his pocket, as after all who would, and it was still there when the police arrested him.

"There he was, fixed nicely. There never was much hope of getting him off—Peter had planted it on him too well for that—and he couldn't say much for himself because he'd got the other murder on his hands and he'd meant to do this one. I told you he hadn't murdered Benson, and he hadn't, but it wasn't for the want of trying."

"But what made Duncan commit suicide?" I asked, with the calm inquisitiveness expected of the interlocutor on these occasions.

"Ah, now you're asking," said Beef. "There were so many things he might have known in that house. He might have known about the old gentleman, he might have known what Stewart was up to, he might have seen him monkeying with the whisky, he might even have realized that Peter returned to the house that evening. But he didn't mean to give anyone in that family away."

I sat thinking over Beef's whole theory. "It seems to me," I said at last, "that you've very little actual proof."

"I'm not saying you're not right," said Beef. "But there's a lot more we could have. There's that bit about the hired car, for instance, we could easy find that out; then old Fryer may not be so silly as he was playing up to be and might be able to tell us a thing or two if he was treated right. I mean, there's a lot more if there was any object in getting it."

"Why isn't there?" I asked innocently.

"Well," said Beef, "I've got funny ideas. But I don't see why I should have Peter hanged for that murder, even if I could prove it. I've told you, he was the nicest old gentleman I've ever met, and I've still got the cup he gave us for that darts championship upstairs. Peter had no means of having those two hanged as they deserved to be, but he wasn't going to let them get away with it."

"Still," I reasoned, "you can't have people taking the law into their own hands in that way."

"Perhaps not," admitted Beef, "only I'm not the law any longer. I'm a private investigator and I'll do as I please. I had the destiny of those two in my hands like marbles, and I chose to let the law take its course without any interference from me. I don't say I've done right and I don't say I've done wrong. I heard from Peter last week. He's married Sheila Benson and he's left for Brazil, where he's starting a new life. Call me what you please, but I didn't mean to interfere with it."

"So you ruined us in the process?"

" 'Ere," said Beef, "don't look at it like that. I mean, this writing of detective novels and following up clues is all very well, but you can't let it interfere with real life and all its varied emotions."

"What have you been reading?" I asked, impressed by this spasm of poetry.

"Something nothing to do with murders," said Beef.

"What made Peter choose you, do you suppose, and why should he have put a detective on at all if he wanted to see his brother hanged?"

"Ah, that's where you come in," said Beef. "You've made such a fool of me in telling the story of those other cases that he thought he was safe in having me. But I got to the bottom of it all right."

"Then," I asked finally, "you really knew the truth all along—before the trial began?"

Beef sucked thoughtfully at the ends of his ginger moustache, looked at me with a slightly pained expression as though wondering whether or not he should tell me the truth, and finally emitted at great length his favourite monosyllable.

"Ah," he said, and he has never enlarged on it.

THE END